Candy-Coated K-Pop

By: Jennifer Tirrell

Dedication:

To everyone who has dreamed of being with a K-pop star . . . or two!

Chapter One

My phone rang as I headed toward the convenience store closest to my office. I intended to pick up something instant before making the long trek home where my cheating fiancé may or may not be right now.

I tucked a long lock of my red hair behind my ear as it fell in my face and pulled the cell from my pocket. It was Ko Minhyuk. One of Korea's hottest actors and my soon-to-be ex-fiancé.

"Why are you calling me now?" I asked him instead of using a normal phone greeting.

He didn't answer right away. In the background, I heard a woman's voice. "Tell her already!"

"Tell me what?" I paused, my hand on the entry door to the store.

"Um . . ." He seemed to gather his courage before continuing, his voice stronger as he said, "Lindsey, I need you to get all your stuff out tonight."

"You need me to do *what*?!" What the hell? As I continued, I slammed my forearm hard into the door in frustration to force it open. "There's no way I can get all my stuff out tonight!"

I met resistance with the door. The sudden stop jarred me. My phone flew from my hand and skittered across the floor inside the store. I looked up and horror spread through me as I realized I'd rammed the door into a customer on the other side.

A customer now drenched in hot, steamy *ramyeon* noodles and broth.

"*Omo!*" I cried out. "I am so sorry!" I reached into my purse, grabbed a tissue, and started dabbing at the yellow and black jacket the customer wore.

I couldn't see his face because of a black face mask and a cap pulled low over his eyes.

He pulled the mask beneath his chin to reveal pink lips just as I realized my phone still sat on the floor with Minhyuk's tinny voice carrying over the sound of the coolers in the store.

"Shit," I cursed and darted over to pick it up. I heard the customer call my name. I had the phone up to my ear with Minhyuk yelling at me as I turned around, not sure I'd heard what I thought I had heard.

"Lindsey, is that you?"

I nearly dropped my phone a second time. "Hold on," I said into the receiver and pulled it away from my ear.

"Jintae?" I said, not believing my eyes. "Ahn Jintae?"

He lifted the cap so I could see his eyes. Those fucking eyes. How long had it been since I'd last laid my own on them?

Minhyuk yelled in my ear again. "If you don't get your shit out of here tonight, it's all getting tossed."

My stomach dropped. Fuck. How was I supposed to do that? Panic set in and I whined, "I can't do that!" Before I could stop myself, I started crying. Then I realized Jintae was talking to me.

"Are you in need of assistance?" he asked me in English. Boy, did those words bring back memories! The memory of the first time Jintae and I met in Japan while in elementary school. The memory of how things used to be between us.

But I had no time to dwell on the past now. I snuffled and said through my tears, "I have no place to go."

Minhyuk must have thought I was talking to him, for he replied, "That's not my problem. Get your shit tonight or it's gone." The phone went dead in my ear as he disconnected the call. I let my arm drop to my side. The tears came in earnest now.

"What am I going to do now?" I cried.

"Lindsey?" Jintae broke through my anguish. "I can help you get your things."

It took me a moment to understand what he said. "Really?" I asked. Did I sound too hopeful? Too desperate?

He nodded.

"But I soaked you in *ramyeon*."

Jintae laughed. "It's okay." He removed his jacket, draping it over his arm. Underneath, he wore a black muscle shirt. My heart jerked in my chest. Those biceps! "It didn't get on me, just my jacket. I'm fine."

7

I cleared my head of dirty thoughts. "I don't want to be a burden."

"It's no trouble, really. My car is parked at my studio a couple blocks that way." He pointed to the right. "Walk with me?"

My tears stopped, but now I couldn't speak, so I nodded and followed him out the door, leaving the clerk to clean up the mess.

Jintae pulled his mask back over his mouth and nose, and we walked in silence down the sidewalk. My mind was a maelstrom of emotion. First, there was the trauma about losing my home and possibly my stuff because of my cheating idiot of a fiancé. And then there was the shock of running into someone from my past who I'd rather forget existed.

The last time I'd seen Jintae, he'd been towering over me laughing as I lay sprawled on the floor of the cafeteria in high school, covered in food with my books and papers scattered around me. I'd never returned to that school after that, and I'd returned to the United States shortly afterward.

I was so deep into my thoughts I didn't realize Jintae had been talking to me until he stopped walking and I ran into him . . . again.

"Are you trying to make this a habit?" he asked, his eyes thin lines as he grinned behind his mask.

"Sorry," I said. "What did you say?"

"I asked you how long you've been back in Korea. The last time we saw each other was . . . what? Eleven years ago?" He grimaced at the thought, the corners of his eyes crinkling.

"About that, I think," I replied. "I came back two years ago to live with Minhyuk." Now it was my turn to grimace.

"Where did you meet him, anyway?" Jintae plowed on, oblivious to my discomfort.

"Oh, uh, on the set of a movie he was filming in California. I was the set photographer. I worked with him quite a bit as I took a lot of photos for the movie." I thought reminiscing would hurt, but it wasn't as bad as I thought it would be. I even smiled. "It amazed him that my Korean was so good. We hit it off right away and he asked me to move to Korea with him. He even helped me start my business here." My thoughts turned dark. "I thought we'd be forever."

"I'm sorry. I shouldn't have . . ."

"It's okay."

"So, what do you do?"

"Photography still. I shoot promos and behind-the-scenes for dramas as well as photos for use on set. I also do private portrait sessions. How about you?"

He blew air out his nose with a little "humph" sound. "You don't know?" he asked, turning his head to look at me.

I shook my head. "Should I?"

"I'm an idol. Well, I'm solo now, but yeah . . ."

"Idol? Like a K-pop idol?"

"Yeah."

"Wow." I stopped and blinked my eyes. "I had no idea. So you achieved your dream. That's awesome." I kept my voice cheery, but jealousy raged inside me. I'd wanted to be an idol, too. Or rather, a dancer.

We started walking again. "I guess I shouldn't be surprised," I said. "I mean, you were always so artistic in school."

He stopped in front of a deep metallic blue sporty sedan and dug his keys out of his still-damp jacket. The doors unlocked with a *blip blip* sound.

"Nice ride," I said. He opened the passenger side door and threw his jacket over the seat toward the back. Then he stepped out of the way for me to enter. "I'll pay for your jacket. To get it cleaned or replaced." I slipped inside.

"I said, don't worry about it. Buckle up." He slammed the door on my side. I watched him skirt around the front of the car to the driver's side. He folded himself behind the wheel, and I noticed how much taller he was than when I'd last seen him. He had to be at least six feet tall.

"At least let me buy you dinner after this. I haven't eaten yet, either."

He shrugged. "We'll see," he said and took off his mask and cap to expose a perfect pale face with wavy bleached blonde hair. I was not expecting him to be so pretty and my breath caught in my throat. Had he been this beautiful when I knew him before?

His eyes were the same. Mono-lidded, narrow, with irises so dark brown they looked black in the dim lighting of the car. His eyes were so smooth and perfect they seemed carved on his face. They disappeared into straight lines when he grinned.

His nose was a little larger than I remembered and not too pointed. But it was his lips that drew my eyes. They were full and pink and, goddamn, I wanted to kiss them!

10

I licked my own lips and I realized, once again, that he was talking to me. "Huh?"

"I said, where are we going?" He motioned toward the GPS unit built into the dash. "Are you having trouble hearing?"

I scoffed. "No." I rolled my eyes and punched the address into the GPS. As I did so, he opened the center console and took out a bag of hard candy, popping one into his mouth. He offered it to me, but I declined.

Looking at the address, he exclaimed, "Woah. Pyeongchang-dong? High class!"

He put the car in gear and made a quick U-turn.

I sighed and leaned my head back against the seat.

"You okay?" he asked with a concerned glance my way.

"I'll be fine," I said and closed my eyes. What right did he have to be concerned about me?

"You don't look fine," he pressed. "Do you want me to beat him up for you?" The candy clicked against his teeth as he spoke. The car smelled like strawberries.

"Tch." I grinned. "Could you, though? He's a master of a few different martial arts, including *tae kwon do* and *judo*."

"Bah. I could take him easy." Jintae waved at the air and chuckled.

"Look," I said, getting serious. "When we get there, you don't have to come in. I can handle this myself."

"Nonsense. You'll need someone to help with your stuff. Do you have a place to stay tonight?"

"Oh." Shit. I didn't. My best friend, Anne Kim, had a guest over tonight, so I couldn't ask her to take me in. "No."

11

"You can stay at my place. I've got an extra room you can use."

"I don't want to be a burden." I really didn't.

He rolled his eyes at me before focusing on the road again. "Lindsey, you're not a burden."

I sighed and gazed out the window at the buildings flying by us.

"*Ya*. Don't feel bad, okay? He doesn't deserve you."

"You're one to talk," I muttered under my breath. My nervousness made me irritated.

"*Mwo?*" he asked.

"Nothing." I didn't need to bring up our past right now. Not while he was trying to help me.

We rode in silence until he turned the car onto my street . . . or what used to be my street.

"Which one is it?" he asked, slowing. Massive mansions, peeking over high walls, lined the street. Mature cherry trees shadowed the sidewalk that wound along the road. Tears pricked at my eyes. Man, I was going to miss this place.

"Park over there." I pointed to a black wrought-iron gate separating a white stone wall.

"Woah," Jintae said as he pulled in front of my former home. "This place is huge. Damn." He crunched what was left of the candy in his mouth.

"Yeah, well, he *is* the hottest actor in Korea right now. Too bad he's such an asshole." I twisted my lips into a sneer, but the truth was I wanted to cry. *This is my life falling apart in front of my eyes,* I thought.

Jintae turned off the ignition and took the keys out. As I opened the door, I stated again, "You don't need to come with me. Just stay here."

He shook his head and opened his door. "No. I'm coming, too. You shouldn't have to face this on your own."

"I'll be fine," I insisted, but he stepped out anyway. He followed me to the gate. I punched in the code on the security pad, but the gate didn't open.

"Of course, it doesn't work," I muttered, hitting the call button.

"Who is it?" came the tinny reply.

"It's me," I answered. "I'm here for my stuff."

The gate rumbled open. We stepped through and started up the meandering bush-lined brick walkway to Minhyuk's immense home. It loomed over us, two stories high, white and brightly lit to stave off the darkness.

As soon as I stepped onto the porch, the door opened and Minhyuk stood there, arms crossed.

"Who's that with you?" he asked with a frown.

Jintae poked his head around me and waved. "*Annyeong,*" he said, his voice more cheerful than it should have been. "Ahn Jintae-ibnida."

Minhyuk's frown deepened. He glared at me. "K-pop trash? You brought K-pop trash here?"

"*Ya!* Excuse me? What did you just say?" Jintae pushed past me, glaring back at Minhyuk. The two men sized each other up.

"You heard me," Minhyuk replied. "K. Pop. Trash."

13

Jintae looked like he might clock him, so I stepped in between them. "Guys, stop it. Minhyuk, he's just here to help me get my stuff. That's all I want. Then we'll go."

Minhyuk rolled his pretty little eyes and stared down his sharp nose at me. "Since when did you start hanging out with K-pop trash?"

My ex-fiancé hated idols. He swore only entertainers with no talent became K-pop stars.

Jintae muttered behind me, "Say that again, bastard. Call me K-pop trash one more time. I swear."

"Jintae is my friend from before," I said, trying to be as vague as possible.

Minhyuk tilted his head, then burst out laughing. "No shit. Really? All this time you've been hating yourself over K-pop trash?"

"Just let us in to get my stuff," I pleaded, holding Jintae back with both hands. He growled like a rabid dog.

"It's all right there in the foyer." Minhyuk stepped aside. He had this smirk on his face that even I wanted to knock off him.

I grabbed Jintae by the wrist and pulled him through the entryway with me. At the end of the foyer, right where it opened to Minhyuk's massive living room, sat six garbage bags.

"*Ah, jinjja*?!" I cursed, turning to scowl at him. "You put my stuff in garbage bags?"

Minhyuk shrugged. "It was easier that way."

"Or you could have just left my stuff alone and let me deal with it." I sorted through them, trying to get a mental image of what all was there. Luckily, I didn't have much stuff, and so long as my camera equipment and laptop were there, I'd be happy . . . wait . . .

"Uh, Minhyuk, where are my lenses and laptop?"

"Oh. I'm keeping them. After all, I bought it all for you."

Anger ran hot through my veins. "You absolutely did not! I paid for every bit of that stuff. *This* on the other hand . . ." I tugged at the diamond engagement ring and tore it off my finger. "You can have *this* back!" I chucked the ten million won ring at him. It bounced off his right cheek.

Minhyuk cried out and clutched at his face. "Ouch! Bitch. That hurt! I swear to god, if I'm bleeding—" He pulled his hand away, staring at the red on his fingertips. The blood—all except what was dripping from a slight cut under his eye—drained from his face. "I'm bleeding!"

Jintae had gathered up two of the bags and now headed out the door with them.

"Get me the rest of my stuff!" I shouted at Minhyuk, ignoring his frantic cries over the miniscule cut on his cheek.

"You cut me!" he whined. "Now what am I going to do? I have a shoot tomorrow!"

"You should have thought about that before kicking me out of the house and stealing my gear. Now, where is it?"

I heard clicking heels coming from the living room. My first thought was, *He allowed her to wear heels in the house?*

And then *she* stepped through the doorway.

Ji Bong Cha. This drop-dead gorgeous, bitchy-looking Korean goddess with perfect, straight hair down to her ass and a body to die for.

She threw something at my feet. "Is this what you were looking for?" she asked with a sarcastic air of innocence.

The object clattered to a stop at my shoes.

My laptop.

In two pieces.

I could only stare down at it for a moment as my heart dropped to my stomach.

"No," I whimpered. "All my work . . ." I knelt to pick up the pieces, trying not to cry. *I will not show weakness,* I told myself. But, dammit, the tears flowed anyway.

And then Jintae was there, stuffing the broken pieces of my life's works into a bag and shoving it and another bag into my arms. He grabbed the last two himself. "Let's get outta here."

"But my equipment . . ."

"We'll worry about that later. Come on." His voice was soft.

Without another word, we left, Minhyuk once again clutching at his face like I'd bitten off half his cheek or something.

"She only snapped it in two," Jintae said as we walked down the walkway. "Don't worry about it. I have a friend who is good at data recovery. I'll get you a new laptop to replace it."

"But my equipment," I said again.

He stopped at the gate now rumbling open and turned to me. "Lindsey. I told you we'd worry about that later. I didn't want you to have to stay there another minute. He was upsetting you."

We stuffed the bags in the trunk of his car and were soon on our way. He sucked on another piece of candy while I

16

stared out the window. The scent of strawberries filled the interior of the car.

"You okay?" he asked in English, glancing over at me.

I sighed. "Yeah."

"You don't sound okay."

"I'm just . . . I'm just trying to figure out what to do now. I mean, I can't stay with you. I guess I can stay at my studio and sleep in my office."

"You can stay with me as long as you need to."

"What? And cause a career-ruining scandal for you? I can't do that. I shouldn't even stay tonight." I bit back my tears.

He snorted. "Scandal? Please. I'm not worried about any scandal. I'm out of my contract. There wasn't a 'no dating' clause in it, anyway. I can see whoever I want. I'm starting my own company now. It'll be fine. Look, in two weeks I'm going on tour to promote my new album. I'll need someone to watch the condo for me. I'll be gone three months. That'll give you plenty of time to adjust and find your own place. How about it?"

His offer touched my breaking heart. "You'd do that for me?"

He scoffed. "Of course! Why wouldn't I?"

It sounded like a good deal. Besides, what other choice did I have? "All right. I'll do it."

His face broke out in the biggest grin.

Chapter Two

Jintae lived in an upscale condominium just a few blocks from the business district that housed both of our offices.

His condo sat on the second floor of the building. Taking the elevator with our arms full of trash bags, we didn't say much to each other. But he looked like something bothered him.

Finally, he asked, "What did Minhyuk mean when he said you've been hating yourself over K-pop trash?" He seemed a little embarrassed to be asking me, keeping his voice low.

Heat rose to my face. "Oh. I—I don't want to talk about it now." I focused on the floor of the elevator.

"I see," he said, and did not press the matter any further.

When we arrived at the door to his home, Jintae dropped the bags to enter the code for the door. He swung the door open and stepped out of the way for me to enter first.

We kicked our shoes off in the small foyer and stepped up into a short hardwood hall that led to the rest of the condo.

Bright white glass shelving lined the wall to my right. Awards and plaques decorated the shelves.

We turned the corner to the left, heading into his home proper. Jintae started a running dialog.

"This is my bedroom," he said, opening a door at the end of the entry hall.

The room was dark. He flipped on a switch, revealing a neat king-sized bed with a yellow comforter. A dresser stood against the wall opposite the foot of the bed, as well as a large flat-screen television. To the right of the door sat a monstrous sound system. In the far corner of the room, next to the tv, stood another door, slightly ajar.

Jintae walked over to the door and pushed it open. "This is the only full bath in my home."

I peered inside to see a black marble sink with a mirror and a white toilet and walk-in shower.

We moved on. Across the hall was a half bath with just a toilet and sink. Beyond that, the condo opened into a large dining room/living room combo with a kitchen on the left. A good-sized dining room table with six chairs stood across from the kitchen. Beyond it, a white couch rested near the center of the room with a coffee table in front of it. A flat-screen television, larger than the one in his bedroom, took up most of the wall across from the couch. The far wall opened into a floor-to-ceiling window, shrouded in white sheer curtains. In front of it stood another nice stereo system. Cream carpeting covered the floor throughout.

Behind the couch was another door. Jintae opened it and flicked on the light. "Lately I've been using this for storage, but the bed is nice. It has a walk-in closet that leads to the laundry room."

Expecting a cluttered mess, I was pleasantly surprised to see only a few stacks of boxes scattered throughout the room. The bed had records and clothes on it, but they wouldn't be hard to deal with. Jintae moved some of them and we put the trash bags on the bed. There was a dresser I could use against the fall wall.

"Are you hungry?" he asked as I cleared more things away and dug into my bags.

"Starving."

"I'll make us some *ramyeon*. Any preferences?"

"Shrimp, if you have it." It was my favorite.

"I do. Two shrimp *ramyeon* coming up!" He left me to my unpacking.

I closed the door after he left and slid down it, the anxiety from the evening unleashing inside me. I couldn't stop it. I trembled and tears ran down my face as I cried.

What the fuck was I going to do? Part of me wanted to return to the US, but I had my business here and it was booming. I couldn't just leave all of my clients hanging. Plus, the money was good. I had more than enough to live off of, even with the high rental rates in Seoul. The hardest part would be finding an apartment close enough to my studio. Jintae's was in the perfect spot; good apartments in this area were highly sought after and hard to find.

I guess it wouldn't be too bad to stay with Jintae for a while, especially if he wouldn't be here for three months.

But I was more upset that Minhyuk refused to return my camera equipment. Luckily, all of my professional equipment was at the studio. This was my personal equipment. Two camera bodies, a couple tripods, and a myriad of fun lenses I played with in my free time.

I had bought all of these. Not him. They were mine, and I needed to get them back.

Thinking of the equipment reminded me of my laptop. I dug the two pieces out of the bag and cried all over again. That bitch had snapped it right in two. There was no saving it. And I had just bought it about a month ago to work on clients' projects at home. There were two works-in-progress on it, but I'd only backed one up on my cloud. The other was a boudoir shoot, sensitive material that I kept private for my customer. Besides that, though, I had thousands of personal photos that were precious to me.

There came a light knock on the door. I was still wiping my tears away when Jintae eased it open.

"It's ready," he said. I didn't do a good job of getting rid of the signs of my crying, for he asked. "Are you okay?"

I sniffled and held up my laptop. "This is just the least of it," I said. I tried to smile, but really I just wanted to cry again.

"Oh, *ya.*" Jintae rushed into the room and gathered me into a hug. "It'll be okay, Lindsey, I promise. After we eat, I'll call my friend about your laptop. We'll work out the rest. It'll be fine. I promise."

I should have pulled away from him, but I didn't. Instead, the tears started flowing again. I soaked his shoulder. And, god, he smelled like strawberries. I wanted to eat him. Or, at the very least, lick him.

After I quieted, he drew back. "Come on. Let's eat. Don't want the noodles to get cold, *neh*?" He gave me a brief smile and my heart fluttered. I chided myself for feeling that way. I had to remind myself of the atrocities he put me through when we were fifteen.

He took my hand and led me to the dining room table where two steaming bowls of *ramyeon* sat with pairs of metal chopsticks.

My stomach growled as I caught the scent.

Jintae acted the perfect gentleman and pulled out the chair facing the living room for me. He sat in the chair across from me and wasted no time digging into his *ramyeon*, using his chopsticks to pull up big clumps of noodles and slurping them up while they were still hot.

Even after many years in Korea and Japan, I was not that talented. I took smaller chopstick-fuls and blew on them before trying to slurp them up. Minhyuk had always laughed at me for my effort, and Jintae was no different. There was a reason I rarely ate noodles in the company of others.

"You still can't do that right, can you?" he asked and slurped up another big clump of noodles. "See? It's easy."

"I can't," I said. "It's too hot." I blew on my portion and slurped them up . . . kinda.

"You're being too American," he said. "Don't be afraid to be loud and obnoxious. We don't care."

I tried again, this time scooping a bigger clump of noodles out of the bowl. I mean, he was right. Although I'd spent most

22

of my childhood in Korea and Japan, I still ate like a westerner. Plus, I didn't like the hot noodles burning my mouth and throat. Some things I just never learned to do. Or I never learned to do them the right way. Half of the noodles I grabbed slopped back into the bowl, splashing me with broth. I was getting self-conscious now and messing up. Any other night, I would have laughed it off, but after what I'd gone through tonight, I was more inclined to cry instead.

Jintae must have seen my lower lip tremble, for he put his chopsticks down. "*Ya*," he said, his voice soft. "I'm sorry. I know you've had a rough night. I have a fork if that would be easier." He got up and fetched me one without another word, but I was too stubborn to give up. Instead, I went back to eating them the way I'd always done it. Smaller bites. It was slower, but at least I finished, albeit several minutes after he slurped his bowl clean.

Growing up in both Korea and Japan, one of the first things I'd noticed was the way each country ate their food. In Japan, it was common to take your time and savor every bite. While in Korea, eating was more of an inconvenience that interfered with work, so you often ate as quickly as possible.

Jintae waited while I finished, then he brought the bowls into the kitchen to wash them. I walked up behind him intending to take a towel to dry them, but he shooed me away. "I got this. You should finish unpacking and hit the bed. We both need to get up early for work."

I relented and returned to my bedroom. After stuffing a few clothes in the dresser, exhaustion set in, and I abandoned the bags to drop myself onto the bed. I didn't even bother to remove my clothes and was asleep before my head hit the pillow.

Chapter Three

I awoke the next morning to an empty apartment. It was only six am, but Jintae had already left for the studio. He left me a quick note on the dining room table.

Feel free to use my shower and
raid the kitchen if you are hungry.
I'll be working late, so don't wait up.
XOXO
Jintae

I rolled my eyes and smirked. He acted like we were a couple or something. As if!

I walked to my studio after using his shower and raiding his kitchen. The day was sunny and warm, the dust count not too high. It gave me time to think.

I tried to call Minhyuk, but it went straight to voicemail. I groaned. I just wanted to resolve this and get my equipment back.

Anxiety weaseled its way inside me as I thought about the situation and my future. I had an important job in the entertainment industry. Business was great with new clients calling every week, so the last thing I wanted to do was leave Korea. But I needed to find an apartment. Sure, I had three months to figure it out, but I needed to start now if I hoped to find something by then.

It was strange that I now lived with Jintae. We had a tumultuous past I hated thinking about. How had we gone from best friends in elementary school in Japan to enemies in high school in Korea? His selfishness. When he returned to Korea for heart surgery, we lost contact, and when I moved back at the beginning of our freshman year, he hated me. He bullied me and he was the number one reason I left to live with my grandparents in the US. All because he wanted to be popular.

I hated him. No. I shouldn't lie to myself. I didn't hate him. I hated myself for loving him, even though he treated me so badly. I was dumb like that. Maybe that was why I agreed to move in with him. Part of me still loved him.

I shook my head to clear that away. It was nonsense. *You don't love him,* I told myself. *After what he did to you, you hate him.*

I pushed the thoughts out of my head as I reached my studio. I had more important things to consider. Like the increasing number of clients I had. I'd done the photography for Minhyuk's latest drama, which had topped the charts throughout its airing to become the number one watched drama of the year so far. Now everyone wanted me to work on their sets.

When I walked into the reception room of my studio, my secretary and best friend, Anne Kim, looked flustered.

"Thank god you're here," she said. "Have you seen the news?"

"News?" I shook my head. It was nine am. What had I missed?

"We're getting calls right and left. Clients are canceling because of it." She turned her computer screen for me to see right as the phone rang.

My heart dropped as soon as she said, "Clients are canceling." What the hell? The room suddenly got colder.

As the computer screen turned my way, I faced the image of a press conference. A press conference featuring my ex-fiancé and his new girl.

I heard Anne answer the phone but heard nothing after that except what was happening on the screen.

"The last time I saw her," Minhyuk said, "She was leaving in the company of a K-pop idol, Ahn Jintae."

My jaw dropped to match my heart. Was he insinuating what I thought he was insinuating? I sank into the chair usually reserved for clients as my knees buckled.

He looked heartbroken. That bitch, Ji Bong Cha, rubbed his back.

My blood boiled as it raged through my veins. How dare he do this to me!

"Lindsey? Lindsey!"

Anne calling my name snapped me back to the office. "Huh?"

27

"We just lost another client. They think you're responsible for this. They think you cheated on him."

The glare I gave her shut her up. "I did not do this," I seethed. "This was not my fault! He dumped me. Last night. He . . . he . . ." I started shaking. What the actual fuck was Minhyuk doing to me?

"Oh, honey." Anne rushed around her desk to embrace me. "Minhyuk did this?"

I nodded. "He dumped me. I did nothing to him."

"What about the footage of you and Ahn Jintae?"

"Footage? What footage?"

"Of you two leaving Minhyuk's place together. Oh, and leaving a convenience store, too."

"He shared that? Oh gods . . ." I covered my face with my hands. "We're old friends. I ran into him last night. He helped me get my stuff. That was it." I didn't mention to her that I'd stayed at his condo last night.

The phone rang again.

"How many clients have we lost?" I asked before she moved to answer it.

"Five so far," she said, and picked up the phone. "Great Clicks Korea. How may I help you? Yes. Yes, we do . . . today? Let me check real quick. Yes, you can come in today for a consultation. How does eleven am sound? It just opened up . . . Yes . . . Your name?" She tapped away at the keyboard. I found a little solace in the fact that not everyone had canceled, and we were getting a new client.

My cell phone rang. I pulled it from my pocket. It was Jintae.

Chapter Six

Jintae dragged himself through the door shortly before one am. He looked exhausted, but he smiled when he saw me stretch and look his way. Anne had left a couple hours ago.

"*Omo,*" he said. "You waited up for me so late?"

I yawned. "For my laptop actually, but yes."

He had a purple laptop clutched in his arms, and he handed it to me as I stood and stretched again. "Purple?" I asked.

"It's still your favorite color, right?"

My mouth fell open. "You remember that?"

"Of course!" He grinned at me and handed it to me. "Jinju promised me that everything's on there. He transferred it all over, no problem."

I set the computer on the coffee table and popped it open. It started right up, showing my lock screen just as I remembered. I sat on the couch again to experiment with it.

"It's fully charged," he continued. "I've got the power cord in my pack." He swung his backpack around and rummaged through it. "Ah. Here."

I took the cord from him. "You don't know how much this means to me," I said.

"Enough to give me a kiss?" he asked, pointing to his cheek.

My eyebrows went up. "Not a chance."

"Why not?" He pouted and flopped on the couch beside me, so close our thighs touched. Heat flared between us. I inched away until we no longer touched.

"Because I . . ." I stopped myself. I didn't want to unleash on him right now. Not after he'd just helped me with my computer. Instead, I shook my head and pulled up the boudoir photos I needed to finish.

His face popped in front of mine, blocking my view. It startled me and I jumped. My heart kicked into overdrive.

"Because you what?" he asked, a slight smile playing on his face. A smile that made the heat pool in my belly.

My mouth went dry. He smelled so good. I swallowed and pulled my head back, increasing the distance between us. "I-I'm busy," I choked out. "I need to finish this for my client."

He glanced at the screen but made no comment about the photos there. Instead, he looked at his watch. "It's after one am. Don't forget, we have the press conference at nine." He stood and yawned. "I'm going to bed. You should, too."

Shit. I'd forgotten about the conference. Reluctantly, I turned my laptop off and slapped the lid closed.

"Thanks again," I said, picking it up and hugging it to me. The air was charged between us, and I dropped my gaze to the laptop. "It's pretty," I whispered.

I almost expected him to lean down and kiss me. Maybe I wanted him to do it. My heart pounded in my chest.

He blew air out through his nose and when I looked up, I found him staring at me, one side of his mouth pulled up into a half-grin.

"*Kwiyeopda*," he said.

"Huh?" I gave him a blank look. Had he just called me cute?

"Nothing," he said. "Good night."

I had a hard time falling asleep that night.

Chapter Seven

I had set my alarm for seven am, but I heard a tapping on my door before it went off.

Jintae's voice drifted through the door. "Lindsey? Are you awake?"

I grunted and rolled over as the door cracked open. "Not ready," I grumbled.

He laughed. "Well, you need to be. We have to be there at eight to get ready. You know, makeup and all."

I threw back the covers and sat up, rubbing the sleep from my eyes. "What time is it?"

"About six-thirty. I have breakfast if you're hungry. Shower's free, too."

"Six-thirty? Did you sleep at all last night?"

He shrugged. "Ever since the operation, I don't sleep much."

The operation. When we were younger, Jintae had a heart condition that required an operation. He had it done when he was thirteen. Right before all the problems between us started.

I shook the thoughts out of my head. I didn't have time to think about that now. Instead, I climbed out of bed. "Breakfast, did you say?"

"Yeah. You like *kimchi* stew, right?"

I gasped. "I *love kimchi* stew! Remember that time your aunt made some for lunch and we snuck into the kitchen and ate half of it while she was at the store?"

"Ah. Yeah." He laughed. "Good times."

"Your aunt made the best *kimchi* stew."

"Well, I'm not one to brag, but I make a pretty mean pot myself."

I threw on a robe and followed him out to the table, already set up with steaming bowls of stew.

I was impressed. His *kimchi* stew tasted delicious.

As we enjoyed it with rice and *banchan* (side dishes), my phone rang. I froze with the spoon halfway to my mouth. That was Minhyuk's ringtone, the theme song of his most recent *saeguk* drama.

"You okay?" Jintae asked me as I stared at the phone, my eyes wide.

I dropped the spoon into the bowl and picked up the phone. Swiping the Answer Call button, I put it to my ear. "*Yeoboseyo?*"

"Lindsey. I see you're going to do a press release this morning. You better not ruin my career with your lies or there'll be hell to pay."

Minhyuk's words stunned me. The taste of *kimchi* went sour in my mouth. I swallowed hard.

"Lindsey? I know you're there. I can hear you breathing."

45

I cleared my throat. "I-I'm here," I croaked.

"Did you hear what I said?" Minhyuk's voice was bitter.

"Yeah." My heart pounded against my ribcage.

"I mean it. If you ruin my career, all the rest of your stuff is gone. I'll torch it, I swear."

"Please, don't do that, Min . . ." Tears threatened.

Jintae pushed back from the table and came around to my side. "Gimme the phone," he said, snatching it from my hand. "Minhyuk-ssi," he said into the receiver.

I heard my ex's tinny voice as he laughed. "Well, well. If it isn't the K-pop trash."

"Listen here," Jintae continued, unphased by the insult. "If you ever threaten Lindsey again, *you'll* have hell to pay. Just return her things and we'll call it even."

"Not a chance. You two better keep your mouths shut or you'll see just how vindictive I can be." The call disconnected before Jintae could say anything else.

"*Aish*!" he swore. He slammed my phone back on the table and paced back and forth, running a hand through his hair. Noticing the panicked look on my face, he stopped. "Don't worry about him. He's bluffing. He'd never ruin your stuff."

But I shook my head. He didn't know Minhyuk like I did. He was quite capable of carrying out his threat, and I told Jintae that.

"He wouldn't dare," Jintae insisted. "We do the press release as planned. Follow the script. Don't back down. We can't let him get to us, understand?"

I nodded, but I wasn't sure I wanted to do it anymore.

"Go take a shower," Jintae said. "And don't worry."

46

We arrived at Jintae's place of business at 7:45. It was my first time seeing it, and I was impressed. The large, three story building housed his entertainment agency and, according to Jintae, included practice rooms and recording studios along with a small cafeteria, several offices, and the press release room. The PR room sat on the ground floor. Reporters already filed through the entrance.

"This way," Jintae said and guided me past a security desk where the guards bowed as we passed. We headed into a makeup studio down a back hall.

"This is all yours?" I asked, impressed.

"Yep. All That Entertainment. I got the building cheap from another agency that failed. It was already mostly set up the way I needed it to be."

"Nice," I said. And here I felt lucky to lease a solid floor in my building for my business. "It's really beautiful. I like your color scheme."

Purple and yellow graced the walls. He pointed to each color. "You and me." Yellow was his favorite color and purple mine.

I realized what he insinuated. "Bullshit," I said, giving him a playful punch in the shoulder. "There's no way the purple represents me."

He gave me a sheepish look. He almost looked hurt by my jab, and his gaze sought the floor as he tugged his lips up into an uncomfortable smile.

At that moment, a woman came out of the dressing room. "You're here! Come. Let's get you two ready. Time is running short! There's so much to do. *Bballi. Bballi.*" *Hurry. Hurry.* She herded us through the door where chairs and pots of makeup awaited us.

I wasn't used to being all decked out in makeup. I preferred the bare minimum or none at all, since I was always behind the camera.

I blinked my eyes and made faces, much to the delight of Jintae, who took it all in stride. He was used to the flurry of makeup brushes and pads, while I felt like powder was going up my nose. I sneezed a couple times.

The makeup ladies were patient and chatted pleasantly with us as they worked. Jintae told me that Hyerin had been with him since his idol group days and knew her stuff better than anyone. Her assistant, Mijin, was bright and cheery and eager to learn under her *sunbae's* guidance.

Before I knew it, we were hustled into the PR room through a side door at the front where a table sat with two chairs. Microphones sat on the table in front of each. Tables of reporters filled the room, each with a laptop in front of them and a photographer at their side snapping photos as we entered.

I was no stranger to being in front of the press from my time with Minhyuk, but that had been different. I'd sat or stood beside him while he discussed his latest drama, not having to speak except to offer words of support or funny anecdotes.

This, though, was unnerving. After Jintae slid into the far seat, he touched my hand in reassurance below the table when I sat beside him. His manager appeared by his side, standing since there were only the two chairs. He leaned over Jintae's mic.

"I'd like to thank everyone for coming today. On behalf of All That Entertainment, I'd like to welcome you this morning to this news conference, which I hope will clear up some misunderstandings about Ahn Jintae and Miss Lindsey Sullivan. I'll hand it over to Jintae now."

Jintae slid the microphone closer to himself. "Thank you, *sunbae-nim*. Welcome, everyone. I am Ahn Jintae, CEO of All That Entertainment. Yesterday, malicious rumors were spread by actor Ko Minhyuk relating to Lindsey and me. Those rumors are absolutely untrue. I have known Lindsey since our school years when we were best friends. We lost contact in high school after she moved back to the United States, and I had not heard from her until the night of her breakup with Ko Minhyuk a couple days ago. I was not the cause of their breakup. Minhyuk initiated it by kicking her out of the home she shared with him. I did not meet Lindsey until right after this, when we ran into each other at a convenience store. I helped her remove her belongings from his residence and offered her a place to stay at my apartment until she could find a place of her own. Our relationship is purely platonic, and she is going to house-sit for me when I leave for my world tour next week. That's all there is to this situation. Lindsey?"

He looked at me expectantly. At first, I didn't know what to say, but once the words came out, they came freely.

"To say I was shocked when Minhyuk kicked me out of our home is an understatement," I began. "I was completely blindsided. I mean, I knew things were going sour between us, but I didn't expect him to kick me out that night. The night this all transpired, I was walking to a convenience store to get a quick meal before hailing a cab to go home. Ko Minhyuk called me and told me over the phone to remove my belongings. I was so shocked that I accidentally rammed the door into Jintae, spilling *ramyeon* all over him. Before that moment, I hadn't seen him since high school eleven years ago.

"I told him about Minhyuk, and he offered to take me to retrieve my belongings. When we arrived, I noticed he had a girl there. She's the real reason for our breakup. He was cheating on me and wanted me out. Jintae helped me get most of my things from Minhyuk. There's still important items of mine he has refused to release, and my laptop got broken during a heated argument.

"And, yes, Jintae offered, *as a friend,* to let me stay at his place until I can find a suitable apartment. I'll be house-sitting while he's on tour and will have a place by the time he returns. We are not and never have been in a relationship. Jintae is like a brother to me." Okay. That last sentence was a lie, but I refused to spill our whole sordid past to Korea and the world. Instead, I shrugged. "That's all there is to it." But I wasn't done yet. "Ko Minhyuk's lies have ruined my reputation in the photography world. Clients have been dropping me left and right. I just want everyone to know I did nothing wrong. I loved Minhyuk and was always faithful to him. Instead,

Minhyuk wronged me. He cheated, and he lied, leaving me to suffer the consequences. He's the villain here. Not me."

A cacophony of voices filled the room as reporters shouted questions, but Jintae rose, pulling me with him. "I'm sorry. We won't be answering any questions." His manager then escorted us from the room.

After we were in the hallway again, I started shaking as every emotion I'd been holding in suddenly let go. When I couldn't catch my breath and started hyperventilating with tears streaking down my face, Jintae ushered me into his office and asked his manager to get me a bottle of water.

"Here. Sit," he said, guiding me to one of two leather couches that sat opposite each other across a coffee table. He had his hands on my shoulders. His palms were warm.

I sank onto the couch and leaned forward, hiding my face in my hands. He sat beside me and wrapped his arms around me, holding me as I fought to get myself under control.

"*Mianhae*," I whispered once I could speak again. Panic attacks always stole my voice. I took a sip of water his manager had set on the table before he'd discreetly left us.

"You okay now?" Jintae asked, concern marring his pretty face.

I nodded. "Emotional overload. Sorry."

He gave me a comforting smile. "You don't have to apologize. You've been through a lot."

I tugged the corner of my mouth up for a moment. "Thank you. For everything."

"Things may not go back to the way they were. But hopefully they'll help either bring clients back or send you new ones."

"I appreciate everything you've done."

"It's the least I can do."

Uncertainty hit me then. "But what if he retaliates?"

"We'll be ready. Don't worry."

Chapter Eight

I was leaning back on the couch in Jintae's office, nursing a bottle of water, when my phone rang from its place on the table in front of me. The familiar first chords of Minhyuk's drama theme floated through the air. Jintae and I both looked up at the same time.

"Is it him?" he asked from where he sat, staring around the monitor of his desktop computer.

Swallowing, I leaned forward and nodded. My hand reached toward the phone. "Should I?" The moisture left my throat again, leaving it scratchy as I spoke.

Jintae nodded and stood. He walked toward me. "Put it on speakerphone."

"*Yeoboseyo?*" I said into the phone before setting it back on the table. Jintae joined me.

Minhyuk's angry voice filled the room. "What the fuck kind of bullshit was that? I told you not to mess with my reputation."

"I only told the truth," I said, keeping my voice steady although my heart raced in my chest. "You told me not to lie."

"That's not what I asked you to do. You really want me to ruin you, don't you? Because you know I can."

I must have paled visibly, because Jintae put a hand on my knee and leaned toward the phone. "You harm one hair on her head, and I'll sic my lawyers on you, Minhyuk-ssi."

"K-pop trash, is that you?" Minhyuk laughed through the phone. "You think you have better lawyers than I do?"

Jintae scowled but didn't lose his cool. Even so, his fingers dug into the flesh of my knee. "I have the best legal team in the industry. They'd eat you alive, so I'd watch myself if I were you."

"Tch. We'll just see about that." And he cut the connection before we could reply.

I gave Jintae a nervous look. "He's got some damn good lawyers."

The K-pop star waved my concerns away. "The K-pop industry has the toughest lawyers in Korea. Drama lawyers are nothing compared to them." He looked me in the eye. "Remember, Lindsey, you did nothing wrong. He's just trying to scare you."

I sighed. "I know that, but I also know how he can be."

"Just stay true to yourself. I promise it'll all blow over."

My phone rang again. This time it was Anne. I swiped the Answer Call button and put the phone to my ear, conscious that Jintae had not yet taken his hand off my knee. And thinking I rather liked it there.

Before I even got the chance to say hello, Anne was talking my ear off . . . and I couldn't be happier. "Lindsey, is there any way you can come in? I just got a massive influx of calls. Clients rescheduling appointments they'd canceled, new customers, people offering their support. I can't keep up! It's like a madhouse here!"

"I'll be right over," I said, unable contain my excitement. A grin spread across my face.

Jintae noticed and patted my arm. "Sounds like things are looking up."

"Yes! I gotta go. I'll see you later, okay?"

I rose, and he rose with me. "Let me walk you to the door. I'll call you a taxi so you don't have to walk."

"Oh, that's not necessary. It's not like my building is far from here."

"Still. There could be reporters and such. Come on."

❦

I stayed busy the rest of the day, coordinating shoots and talking to new clients. By the time ten rolled around, I was tired and ready for bed. I even hired a new makeup artist to replace Lisa, but she couldn't start until the following Monday, so I was on my own until then. I felt so lucky to have Anne.

By Friday, things seemed almost normal again. Minhyuk had backed off, and I had heard nothing from him over the past few days. That also meant I hadn't gotten my stuff back, either, but I told myself I could live with that for now.

I had seen little of Jintae. He went in early and stayed late at his agency to prepare for his tour. And I was so busy with my work I didn't have time to think about whether I still hated him.

I arrived at my office around six am Friday. I needed an early start for Young Sik's photo shoot. The morning sun would be great for the first round of photos. It was going to be a long day, all reserved for him.

Anne and I collaborated to do Young Sik's hair, makeup, and wardrobe. I forgot how time consuming it was. I would be glad when the new girl started Monday.

The photoshoot went well. We took photos at a local park in the morning, using the low-hanging sun to get good details. Around noon, we stopped for lunch before returning to my office for studio shots. The shoot ended around ten pm in an abandoned factory I'd rented. It was a popular place for photoshoots and action scenes.

Young Sik was a fabulous subject. He rocked all the poses and played the gangster part well. By the time the last shoot ended, we were exhausted and ready to go home again.

I shut off the last of the spotlights. Young Sik helped me carry them to the van, where Anne was busy loading the equipment.

One part of the path was narrow with a wicked drop off to our left. And wouldn't you know that was where I lost my footing in the darkness when I slipped on a pebble.

I dropped the spotlight as I slid down the embankment, my hands tearing when I tried to stop myself. The spotlight tumbled in front of me. It smashed against something somewhere in the darkness. I was more worried about the light than myself—those things were expensive—but then I hit something hard and started to tumble. Now I worried about myself. I couldn't stop my descent.

Luckily, there was a tree at the bottom which stopped me . . . hard. My shoulder and my back hit it, knocking the breath from me with an "Oof!"

I lay there a moment, trying to stop the world from spinning.

I heard a shout above me, and Young Sik landed beside me, crouching and peering at me with a worried look on his face. "Are you okay? Can you stand?"

I shook my head to clear my vision. I barely made him out in the gloom. "I-I think I'm okay," I said and attempted to sit. He guided me with his hands until I leaned against the tree. I felt myself all over. Nothing appeared to be broken, though my hands and knees stung from scrapes.

"Are you sure?" he asked. His hand lay on my shoulder. Why was it sending tingles through me?

I shook it off and nodded. "Help me up?" I asked. He pulled me to my feet, but I lost my balance and fell against the tree trunk, taking him with me.

Our bodies collided in a spark of fire. His hands planted on either side of my head. Our lips were mere inches apart. When I looked up, his eyes gazed into mine with a wonderment that made my insides melt. I ran my tongue over my lips to moisten them. I could scarcely breathe. God, he smelled *so* good. Like earth and expensive cologne. And the hint of chocolate.

He studied my face, his gaze searching out all the details. His lips inched closer to mine.

"Lindsey!"

Anne's voice crying out from above sent us scattering. My heart beat so hard I thought I might faint. Oh god. I almost kissed a client. He almost kissed me!

Young Sik cleared his throat. "D-do you need help climbing back up?"

Then from above, "Are you all right? Did you fall?"

I called back, "I did! I'm fine, though."

Young Sik pushed me toward the incline. "Let's go," he whispered. I nodded.

By the time we made it back to the van, my palms were stiff from the scrapes. Anne gasped when she saw them and the torn pants around my bloody knees. "We need to get you to a hospital."

I froze. "I-I'm fine. I got worse playing in the woods as a child." I tried to laugh it off, but I hated hospitals. "I just need to clean myself up."

Anne gave me a look. "You know that's not how we do things in Korea. A doctor will do a better job cleaning your cuts so they don't get infected."

And that's how I ended up staying in a hospital until midnight with my assistant and a K-pop star.

Chapter Nine

Saturday morning, I woke up stiff and tired. I didn't have any appointments until three, which made me happy. Saturday was always a late day, and I wasn't open on Sunday.

When I crawled out of bed, I checked the bandages on my hands and knees. How I'd missed injuring my face, I'll never know, but I was thankful for that. Especially since Young Sik and I had come so close to . . .

I wiped that memory from my head. What the hell had I been thinking, almost kissing a client like that?

I picked up my phone and checked it for messages. I had one from Anne and one from Young Sik.

Young Sik?

Curious, I tapped on it.

In Korean, he'd typed: *Just checking up on you. Hope you are okay. If you can't get the photos done by Sunday, don't worry about it. Stay healthy!*

I felt one of those silly smiles creeping up on my face. The ones you get when you're in love and your boyfriend texts you something sweet. Fuck. What was I thinking? Stop it, brain!

I shot him a quick reply: *Thank you. I'm fine. There shouldn't be a delay with the photos. I'll text you when they're ready.*

Anne had sent one asking if today's shoots were still on. She was worried about my hands. I assured her I'd be fine. It was only two shoots and they were both studio appointments, so I figured they wouldn't be a problem.

In the meantime, I had to get started on Young Sik's photos. I'd taken over three hundred of them in all. I'd be busy for a while. I wanted to give him an abundance to pick through for his album.

But first, a shower. I'd arrived before Jintae last night but had been too tired to even think about showering. And now, here it was nine am and I felt sticky and disgusting from my fall. The hospital had cleaned my wounds and wiped off most of the dirt and debris from my skin in their search for more injuries, but I still felt unclean.

The condo was empty. Jintae had already left. I hadn't seen him much these past few days since the PR event. He was super busy getting ready for his tour, leaving early every morning and arriving home well after midnight.

I didn't know what to think about him anymore. After all those years of me hating him (or hating myself) for his bullying, he seemed to have changed. There were times I caught him looking at me like he wanted to devour me, often while sucking on that damned strawberry candy of his. And the way he touched me so comfortably. It sent delicious shivers along my spine. I wanted him to touch me more.

I turned on the shower, checked the water temperature, and stepped under the warm stream. Stealing some of Jintae's strawberry shampoo, I lathered my hair.

And what of Young Sik? Heat flashed through me as I thought of our almost-kiss last night. I had to admit that taking photos of him in those sexy gangster outfits made me wet. And I wasn't one to fall for my clients. Not. At. All. Well . . . besides Minhyuk. Hmm. Maybe I wasn't as reserved as I thought.

I rinsed the shampoo and dirt from my hair while pondering this. When was the last time I'd had sex? I was probably just deprived, so both of these K-pop boys were affecting my starving libido. Before this, Minhyuk had been gone for three months, filming his newest drama, a *saeguk*, alongside the very woman he was with now, so he hadn't been in Seoul for a while. And when he'd returned two weeks ago, he'd looked tired and seemed to want his space, so I had given it to him, thinking I was just being a considerate fiancée. But then he'd become irritable toward me, blaming me for the littlest things, picking out flaws we both knew I had, and making my life miserable. I had begun to suspect something was going on with him. That he had someone on the side, but I'd had no proof . . . until the night I ran into Jintae and all hell broke loose. So I hadn't had sex in four months. No wonder these two boys excited me!

My hands and knees didn't look so bad after washing them. After I finished showering, I put band-aids on the worst of the scratches and sat at the dinner table in my robe with my long, red hair bundled up in a towel and started working on Young Sik's photos.

Slipping into my work made time pass quickly and before I knew it, it was time to get ready for work. I didn't want to stop, though! Editing photos of Young Sik made this huge smile spark on my face I swear I kept the whole time I worked on them.

❤ 🦋

After I got out of work that evening, I window-shopped a few of the stores still open along my route. One was a bakery with a window filled with luscious sweets. On a whim, I decided to treat myself, and I purchased a fluffy lemon meringue pie. When I got home, I put it in the fridge for later, then ordered delivery chicken to eat while I worked on Young Sik's photos.

I was so deep into editing that I didn't notice midnight had come and gone until Jintae stumbled in through the door. He looked exhausted, but he still gave me a smile when he saw me sitting at the table surrounded by chicken bones and my laptop.

"You're not getting it sticky, are you?" he asked, leaning over my shoulder. "Oh. Who's that?" He pointed at the screen.

"Young Sik. He's a—"

"I know who he is. I mean, why is he on your computer?" Was that jealousy I saw on his face?

"He's a client. I did a photoshoot for his first solo album. He's doing it all himself, you know."

Jintae waved a dismissive hand. "Then why were you staring at him all fangirly when I walked in?"

"I didn't—I wasn't . . . Jintae! He's a client!" Oh god, had he seen me doing that? My face heated.

He grinned at me. "You don't need him. You have me." At this point, his face was right next to mine and I leaned to the left to put distance between us. When I made eye contact, his grin widened. I rolled my eyes and laughed, not sure how else to react. He patted my shoulder and headed into the kitchen.

"Did you save any chicken for me?" he asked, sticking his head in the fridge. "Ooh! Pie!"

"You can have a slice if you like."

"Eh, no. Thanks. I mean, I wanted chicken." He threw me a pouty look. "But I guess I'll settle for some reheated *kimchi* stew."

He sat across from me with his steaming bowl of stew and poked out his lower lip. "I can't believe you didn't buy me any chicken." But he had a sparkle in his eye that made me laugh.

"I'll get some for you tomorrow, cry baby. Just promise me you'll come home early so it won't be cold."

"Deal!" he said with a grin before stuffing his face with stew.

I went back to my photos. After a few minutes of clicking in silence, I peeked over the laptop screen to find Jintae asleep with his arms crossed on the table.

"Jintae," I said. "*Ya.* Why don't you go to bed?"

He mumbled something and snuggled deeper into his arms, his unruly blonde locks swirling around him. Damned if the sight of him didn't strike me right between my thighs. Here we go again with the misdirected sexual desire.

Remember, you hate him, I chastised myself. But why did I want to brush the wispy locks away from his face?

I couldn't concentrate on my photos anymore, so I closed the program and shut down my laptop, leaving it on the table.

I walked around to the other side and touched Jintae's shoulder. "*Ya.* Get up and go to bed."

He raised his sleepy head, looking at me like a fluffy, confused kitten. "Oh. Yeah."

Instead of heading toward his room, he followed me to mine. "Your room is that way," I reminded him and turned back to open my door.

His arms snaked around me from behind. "I wanna sleep with you tonight," he murmured in my ear, sending delicious shivers down my spine I could not ignore. "Just like when we were little. Remember?"

I remembered. We each lived with our aunts while in Japan, and our aunts were best friends, so we spent a lot of nights together. If Jintae was having a bad night with his heart acting up, he'd slip into my bed and fall asleep against my back. He always told me pressing his heart against me helped it settle.

Now, here he was, pressing against me once more.

"Is your heart bothering you?" I asked.

"Mm," he replied, his lips vibrating against the skin of my neck, making me shiver.

I chewed my lip, thinking. My heart thudded in my chest. What could it hurt? "Come on, then."

He followed me obediently into the bedroom, stripping to his boxers as he approached the bed. I was in my pajamas, so I crawled in bed and put my phone on the charger on my nightstand. Jintae slipped beside me. I turned away from him, and he snuggled against me, wrapping his arms around me and pulling me close. "You smell good," he whispered, burying his face in my hair.

To be honest, he did, too. He always smelled like strawberries, and it drove me mad.

I hate him, I reminded myself. *I hate him for what he did to me.* But then he nestled even closer to me and let out a little sigh.

My heart melted.

Chapter Ten

I awoke to the sun streaming into my bedroom and Jintae's arm draped over me. When I moved my head to check the time on the wall clock, that arm tightened around me, making my heart flutter.

Then I noticed the time. It was 8:17 and Jintae was still asleep beside me. He was always awake and often gone when I finally dragged myself out of bed on Sundays. Why was he still sleeping?

I turned my head and shoulders just enough to see him. He had pulled his head away from me with his other arm tucked under it. His eyes were closed.

"Jintae," I whispered. He made a little mewling noise and brought his face against me again, rubbing against the back of my head like a cat as he tightened his grip on me. His eyes remained closed. "Jintae, it's after eight. Are you late for work?"

One eye popped open, and he eyed me with suspicion. "*Jinjja?*" he asked. *Really?*

"Yeah. *Jinjja,*" I replied, pointing to the clock on the wall.

He lifted his head and squinted, then bolted into a sitting position. "Shit! What day is it?" The blankets fell from his bare chest, revealing an ugly scar over his heart. It drew my eyes, and I couldn't look away.

"S-Sunday," I replied, distracted. I wanted to touch it.

He noticed me staring and looked down at himself. "Oh. You haven't seen it yet, have you?"

I tore my eyes away from the scar and averted my gaze. "I'm sorry. I didn't mean to stare."

"It's okay. You can touch it if you want. It doesn't hurt."

I reached toward him and he suddenly grabbed my hand. "*Omo*! What did you do to yourself?" He rubbed his thumb over the scrapes on my palm.

"I fell during a photoshoot. I'm okay though. Just a few scrapes here and on my knees."

He drew my hand to his lips and, much to my chagrin, kissed my palm. I jerked my hand back in surprise. "Aren't you going to be late for work?"

"It's Sunday. I'm not all that worried about it. I gave everyone the day off. I just have a few odds and ends to work on. No biggie." He stretched and flopped back beside me. As he did so, he grabbed me and pulled me on top of him.

I squealed as he tickled me like he used to do when we were kids. He was always a touchy-feely person.

I started out on my back, stretched across his chest with my legs kicking in the air. Then I squirmed until I faced him. My gaze moved to his lips. Those luscious lips.

He pursed them and my gaze slid up to the narrow slits of his eyes. They held a look of pure mischief.

Jintae leaned toward me, but I shied away. There was no way I was going to let him kiss me. I scrambled to my feet on the floor, my heart racing.

"I-I need to go to the bathroom," I sputtered and nearly fell over my own feet as I skedaddled out of the room.

Once I reached the bathroom, I slammed the door shut and slid down it until my ass hit the cold tile, holding a hand to my heart to still its beating.

I'd almost given in. I'd almost let him kiss me. Fuck fuck fuck. Why was there an army of butterflies in my stomach? Why did my heart flutter so? Not him. There was no way I'd let it be him. He couldn't charm me that easily.

A knock sounded on the door. His voice came, muffled by the wood. "Lindsey? You okay?"

"I-I'm fine," I called to him.

"I'm gonna get ready for work, then. If I don't see you before I go, don't forget you promised me chicken tonight. I'll be home around seven."

"Okay. I won't forget." I feigned nonchalance and stayed in the bathroom until he left.

When the apartment was quiet, I took a shower, threw on some jean shorts and a short-sleeved blouse and took a walk around the block before settling to work on the photos.

When fully engrossed in my work, the hours could fly by like minutes. That's how it suddenly became five pm and I hadn't stirred an inch as I worked, letting only my hands and the mouse do everything.

And then I came to the final photo. I let out a gasp as I gazed at it. It was perfect. Perfect lighting, perfect shadows, perfect everything. And it made my core turn to molten lava.

Most of the image was shrouded in darkness. I'd taken it in the abandoned factory right before we packed up to leave. A spotlight outside shined through a window above Young Sik, highlighting the best parts of him. He wore a fine 1930s black pinstripe suit with a black fedora. Most of his face was in shadow, leaving only the bottom half visible. He had a wicked grin on his face, like he was about to do something sinister. I barely made out his eyes peeking from beneath the hat's brim, adding to the noir quality of the photo. A gold watch gleamed on his arm as his hand tipped the fedora.

I loved it. It took minimal editing to make it even better. I was so pleased with it I printed out a copy for my album of special photos, mostly ones that had won awards or had been in notable dramas.

All I could think of was this man was a sex god, and I'd almost kissed him that night. Damn that Anne for ruining everything. I tittered at the thought, though. I loved Anne. She was my best friend, even if she had horrible timing.

I put the album back in my room, thankful that Minhyuk hadn't destroyed it. Then I returned to the table to transfer the photos to a jump drive for Young Sik. I sent him a quick text to let him know the photos were ready. It took him several minutes to respond.

Sorry. I'm at my folks. I can pick them up around 9. Is that okay?

Sure! No problem! Enjoy your family time, I responded and sent him my address.

I continued to work on other photo shoot pictures until Jintae came home at seven. We ordered chicken and I forgot all about Young Sik coming.

The awkwardness of the morning resounded in my memory, but Jintae was back to his normal, jubilant self.

"Thanks for the chicken. It was delicious!" he said, licking his lips. "I'm going to take a shower. Shall we sleep together again tonight? I haven't slept that good since . . . well, since probably before my operation. You are good for my soul." He gave me a warm smile that turned into a mischievous grin, turning my insides to lava once more.

I cleared my throat, trying to push the naughty thoughts conjured by my brain back into oblivion. "I . . . I think I'll have some of my pie."

"You do that," he said and disappeared into his room.

Chapter Eleven

I looked up from taking a bite of my lemon meringue pie.

Jintae leaned against the wall, his blonde hair still damp and tousled from towel-drying it after his shower. He was shirtless, the scar over his heart visible above his crossed arms. A yellow sweatshirt lay draped over his forearms. He rolled something around in his mouth, probably a piece of strawberry candy. The sound of it clicking against his teeth had caught my attention.

My gaze raked across his lithe figure. His grey sweatpants hugged his slender hips as he stood. He watched me with an amused look on his face, his eyes dancing in the light, a smile playing on his succulent lips.

"Is something funny?" I asked, setting my fork on the plate. I attempted to look calm, but my blood raced through me, pumped by a heart in overdrive. If I hated him so much, why did I feel this way?

It took real effort to keep my breathing some semblance of normal. And even then, I was doing a shitty job. My eyes felt dilated and wider than they should be. Why did he do this to me?

He walked toward me, drawing the sweatshirt over his head. He shrugged into it and stood at the opposite side of the table.

Instead of answering me, he widened his grin, his eyes scrunching into tiny thin lines. His tongue fondled that piece of pink candy behind even pinker lips. The temperature of the room rose several degrees.

"Is it good?" he asked instead.

"Huh?" The question caught me off-guard.

"The pie. Is it good?"

"Oh. Mmm. Very good." I picked up the fork again and shoved another bite of pie into my mouth. The sweet tartness returned me to my senses . . . until he started rolling the candy around with his tongue again. All I pictured was him doing that to me.

I mentally slapped myself. *You hate him,* I reminded myself. But my walls were crumbling. And his goddamned candy fixation wasn't helping matters any.

He leaned toward me. Abruptly, I pushed my chair back and stood, all sorts of scenarios running through my head. What did he want? Was he going to try and kiss me again like this morning?

He laughed, straightening. "Relax. I was just going to ask for a bite of your pie." His gaze fell on me, on my wide eyes and my mouth open like a little "o." He cocked his head. A wicked grin spread across his face. "Are you—?"

"No!" I gasped, not giving him the chance to complete his sentence. I held up a hand to stop him from coming any closer to me as he walked around the table. *Horny,* I thought. He was going to ask me if I was horny.

Before I knew what was happening, he grabbed my wrist and used it to push me until my back hit the wall. He stood so close to me I smelled the scent of strawberries on his breath. He pressed his body against mine to hold me in place. I tried to keep my breathing normal, but I failed miserably. My breath hitched as he leaned toward my left ear. His lips brushed the lobe as he whispered, "Do you want me to kiss you?"

I tried to resist, I really did, but the scent of him overpowered my thoughts, rendering me helpless. Strawberry soap, strawberry shampoo, strawberry candy. Oh god, he smelled like a strawberry temptation dessert. All I could do was nod and squeeze my eyes closed.

His lips touched mine. They were soft. He let go of my wrist and slipped his hand beneath my chin, tilting my face to get at my lips better. I tasted the candy on his lips. Kissing him was like kissing a strawberry-flavored marshmallow.

He drew back and shifted the candy in his mouth, crushing it between his teeth. When our lips touched again, he teased my mouth open. His candy-coated tongue darted inside. The strawberry flavor mixed with the lingering taste of lemon from my pie.

Usually, I like nothing other than food in my mouth. No tongues, no dicks. But this . . . this was different. Orgasmic, even. I couldn't get enough. I could have deep throated his tongue if it had been long enough.

My hands twisted in the fabric of his sweatshirt as I fought to control myself. When he finally drew back, he left me breathless. *We* were breathless.

His eyes searched my face. His hair had curled at the tips from drying. It was sexy, and it turned me on, especially with the way he now looked at me, his eyes heavy lidded, his mouth slightly open. He ran his tongue across his lower teeth.

"I want to taste you," he breathed.

"You already did," I said, oblivious to what he was implying.

"No. I want to taste *you*. All of you." His eyes traveled the length of my body, stopping at the zipper on my shorts before moving back up to my face. I gasped as I caught his meaning. "May I?"

I swallowed and gave a little nod. I mean, we'd gone this far, what was a little farther, right?

He laid sweet marshmallow kisses on my cheeks, my jaw, my neck, then proceeded to trail further down my body. He unbuttoned my blouse, kissing my cleavage. I let out a gasp as his lips touched a nipple through the satin material of my bra. With a quick flick of his fingers, my breasts popped free. He suckled my nipples, one at a time. The heat from his lips lit me on fire. I moaned as my center flared and my insides became all melty.

He sank to his knees, trailing kisses as he moved. I gasped when he stuck his tongue in my belly button. Further down he went, touching his lips to my waist just above my shorts. His deft fingers made quick work of the button and zipper. My shorts dropped to the floor.

He feathered his lips across the fabric of my panties. His fingers traced along the lace edging. A finger slipped underneath the fabric at my inner thigh, seeking my wetness. Another gasp escaped me.

Jintae looked up at me as he slid my panties down my legs to the floor. I wanted to step out of them and my shorts, but I was afraid to move. I teetered on the edge of an orgasm and the slightest movement could set me off. My breathing came in ragged bursts as I peered down at him.

Oh god, what was I doing? Why was I letting him do this?

But I could not help myself.

He rolled his head so his cheek lay against the sensitive skin of my upper thigh. His tongue darted out. He held it there and watched me to see my reaction.

His tongue touched my hot flesh, and he pivoted so he kneeled in front of me again. His fingers spread my folds, and he flicked his tongue across my clit once . . . twice . . . His mouth covered me. When he began to suck, it was over for me. I came hard, pressing myself against him as his tongue caressed my nub.

"Fuck me," I cried out, my hips rocking against his face. "Oh god!"

I think he took my exclamation for an invitation. Before the last aftershock rolled through me, he was standing again, his sweatpants tossed aside. He rubbed his hardness against me, bringing yet another orgasm as he thrust himself inside me.

He was thicker than I expected, filling my swollen hole. I shuddered and grabbed his bare cheeks beneath the sweatshirt, keeping him close to me. He thrust inside me, slowly at first, then faster and faster. His breathing escalated with every thrust. He had his forearms braced against the wall on either side of my head. His forehead touched mine. Our gazes locked together. Every breath he exhaled smelled of sex and candy. It was exhilarating. It didn't take long for another orgasm to rock my body . . . or maybe it was a continuation of the previous one.

My insides squeezed around his cock as the waves of pleasure hit me. He thrust faster, harder, pounding into my tender flesh. His breath came in ragged bursts now, his thrusts erratic until he stiffened and came inside me with a muffled groan.

Jintae remained still for a bit, waiting for his breathing to calm before peeling himself off the wall. He pulled out of me and stood, his eyes catching mine.

"Goddamn," he said. "I think I blew the top right off it." He swiped his now sweaty hair back from his face. "I need another shower. The fuck did you learn all that?"

"All what?" I asked, an innocent smile on my face.

"All the squirming and the gripping and the . . . the quaking. What a ride!"

"Just a natural, I guess," I said with a shrug.

And then, the intercom buzzed.

Chapter Twelve

O h shit. I'd completely forgotten about Young Sik. I made a mad dash for the bathroom to clean myself up, leaving Jintae to answer it.

His voice came through the bathroom door. "Lindsey . . . why is that dude you were drooling over on your laptop standing outside my building, ringing my door?"

Did I sense jealousy in his voice? "He's my client!" I answered. "Please let him in. I have photos for him."

"I thought I told you I didn't like strange men in my apartment."

I cracked the door. "Did you? I'm sorry. I wasn't thinking. I did this all the time at Minhyuk's if a client was in a hurry to get their stuff. I won't do it again. Just let him in, please?" I gave him my best *aegyo* look and batted my eyes. "Pwetty pwease?"

He sighed, the ghost of a smile gracing his lips. "Just this once, okay?" He pointed at me. "You're lucky you're so cute!"

"Kamsahabnida!" I exclaimed and slammed the door shut again. *Thank you!*

Quickly, I cleaned myself using a washcloth, and I buttoned my shirt back up. By the time I figured I was presentable, I heard the doorbell ring. Jintae answered it as I stepped out from the bathroom.

The two men came around the corner, and I gave Young Sik a polite bow. "Your photos are right in here. Come on. I'll get them for you."

He shuffled behind me, his slippers scuffing on the hardwood floor. Jintae stood by the kitchen, watching us, his arms crossed. Every time I glanced at him, he looked like he wanted to stab Young Sik with a chopstick.

I handed Young Sik the jump drive, then clicked on the photo folder on my laptop so he could see what he was getting. He clicked through the edited versions, stopping now and then with a "Woah" or a "Wow" whenever one caught his eye. When he came to the last one, he stopped a moment, staring at it.

"This," he said. "I think this one will be my album cover. It's perfect. Wow. You did . . . I mean . . . I'm blown away by your work. Thank you." He bowed to me and I bowed back.

"It was an absolute pleasure," I said. "Thank you for taking a chance with me."

Jintae walked over, scoffing. "Don't sell yourself short. You do an amazing job. The risk is minimal." He moved behind me and put his arm around my waist, much to my horror. I almost expected him to place a kiss on my cheek. Embarrassed, I pushed his hand away and stepped away from

78

him. Young Sik watched our exchange with curiosity, his head cocked.

"Are you two——?"

"No."

"Yes."

Jintae and I tried to answer at the same time, confusing our guest even more.

"We are not dating," I insisted, giving Jintae a pointed look.

"I should go," Young Sik said as Jintae stepped toward me again.

"I'll walk you out." I dodged Jintae and headed toward the door with Young Sik. Once we were outside the condo and heading toward the elevator, I said, "We're not together." Why did I feel the need to assure him of that?

Young Sik smiled. "Thanks again for everything. If you want, I'll stop by your office after I get the album designed so you can see what it looks like."

"Oh! That would be wonderful," I exclaimed.

The elevator dinged, and the door slid open. We entered the car.

"You did a wonderful job with the photos. Thanks again." Young Sik looked uncomfortable standing next to me, shifting his feet as he stared at them.

"Thank you," I said, trying to put him at ease. "I hope Jintae didn't irritate you."

"He seemed a little . . . possessive."

"He's just a friend. I'm sorry if he offended you."

"Nah. It's okay. I just wanted to make sure you were available." The doors opened, and he stepped out. "I can go from here. See you around."

I was too shocked to say anything. He wanted to make sure I was available? My mouth dropped open as I watched him shuffle toward the front door with that easy-going gait of his. Did he just——? Was he interested in me?

The elevator closed on my toes as I watched him go. I yelped and jumped back so the doors could close.

What the actual fuck? My lips tipped up into a grin. Oh. My. God. Young Sik liked me!

When I returned to the apartment, Jintae was clicking through the photos on my laptop, a scowl on his face.

"What are you doing?" I asked, crossing my arms.

He looked up. The scowl disappeared. "Oh. You're back."

I tapped my foot. "Why are you going through my laptop?"

He backed off, holding up his hands. "I was just looking at the photos. He looks like a pompous ass."

I snorted. "Okay?"

"Did you see the way he was looking at you? He was practically fucking you with his eyes."

"Jintae!" My face heated.

"What? It's true. I mean, look at what you're wearing."

I looked down at myself. I wore the same white blouse and jean shorts I'd been wearing when Jintae himself thrust me up against the wall and fucked me. I shrugged. "And?"

He glared at me. A low growl emanated from his throat.

"Omo!" I covered my mouth with my hand. "You're jealous!"

"I am not."

"You are, too. Just look at you." I started laughing. "You think you claimed me tonight, and now you're jealous because another man invaded your territory."

"*Ya!* Shut up already." He stuck his hands in the front pocket of his hoodie and trudged toward his room. That made me laugh even harder. Turning back around, he stalked toward me.

"Wh-what are you doing?" I backpedaled toward the couch in the living room behind us.

His face split into that mischievous grin. "Where are you going?" he asked. "You're not afraid of me, are you?"

"Jintae, that's not funny." The backs of my legs hit the sofa, and I lost my balance, flipping over the arm and onto the couch. He was on me in a hot minute, straddling me and holding my hands above my head, all while grinning at me like a madman. It made my pulse race.

The overpowering smell of strawberries invaded my nostrils, bringing up the memories of what had happened between us right before Young Sik had shown up.

You're angry at him, I told myself. *You hate him.* And yet, I still couldn't get myself to say those words aloud.

He leaned in close. "You owe me. For inviting another man into my home." The grin widened. My heart throbbed.

"What are you going to do with me?" I asked, more in anticipation than fear. But, fuck, I'd just told Young Sik we weren't together, and yet, here I was craving his touch again. I had to get out of this.

His lips came close to mine, and he brushed them against me. A moan escaped my mouth, and he plunged his tongue inside. I couldn't resist. I pushed myself into the kiss, my body igniting wherever our skin touched.

Then the vision of my last day of school pushed its way into my thoughts. Me, on the floor of the cafeteria, humiliated and soaked in stew with Jintae looming over me. It was so vivid I could smell the *kimchi*. I flinched and pulled my face away.

"Jintae, stop," I whispered. I struggled to free my hands. "Let me go."

I believe he thought I was playing, for he tried to kiss me again, but I bucked beneath him. Terror trickled through my veins, turning my body cold. Suddenly, I couldn't move. I couldn't breathe.

"Stop it!" I cried. My eyes burned with tears.

He stopped. The weight lifted, and he was beside me, lifting me and cradling my head against his chest. "I'm sorry," he whispered. "I'm sorry."

I clawed at him in my terror, hot tears burning my cheeks. What was happening to me? Another panic attack?

He held me until I calmed.

"Are you okay?" he asked after I became still.

I shook my head. No, I wasn't okay. I had to tell him. I had to let him know.

"I hate you," I muttered. "I hate you so much, Jintae, that I don't know what to do." And I started crying all over again.

Chapter Thirteen

I *hate you.*

Those three words hung in the air between us. Jintae stared at me, open-mouthed, like I'd slapped him in the face.

"Why?" he asked. "Why would you hate me? I'm not Minhyuk. It's me, Jintae."

He thought I was having some sort of flashback to Minhyuk. "I know it's you," I said, tears blurring my vision.

"Then why . . . why do you hate me?" His words escaped on a quiet breath.

I struggled out of his embrace and stood. I wasn't ready to discuss this. I *couldn't* discuss it.

"Lindsey?" His face had fallen. I had hurt him. I had hurt him and it was tearing me apart. My heart shredded.

"I'm sorry," I whispered. I turned and fled to my room, where I slammed the door shut and collapsed on the floor, unable to move a step further. Fresh tears spilled down my cheeks.

Fuck. Here I was again, putting his feelings before my own. Just like I'd done way back in high school when I'd blamed myself for the change in his attitude toward me. That I needed to try harder. To do better for myself. . . no, to do better for *him*.

A light rap made me turn my head toward the door.

"Lindsey? Are you okay? Whatever I did, I'm sorry. Did I come on too strong tonight? I'm sorry. I thought you felt the same."

He sounded pitiful. I pictured him standing at the door with his forehead pressed to the wood.

What could I say? I didn't even know how to express how I felt. Would he even remember? Would he even care?

He knocked on the door again. "Won't you talk to me? Are you mad because of Young Sik?"

I drew in a shaky breath. "No," I whispered. Then louder so he could hear. "No, I'm not mad about that or about this evening."

He turned the knob and peeked in. "What is it then? Are you okay?"

I looked up at him from the floor, devastation flooding me. "Jintae, you . . ." *Come on, girl, spit it out.* "You ruined my dream."

He gave me a confused look. "Because of Minhyuk? I was only trying to help."

"No, not that. I-I've hated you for a long time because you made me give up dancing." There. I said it. I dropped my eyes to my lap, wringing my hands. After all these years, I finally said it.

"Huh?" Jintae squatted in front of me. "What do you mean? How did I do that?"

"You don't remember?" Tears threatened again. Of course, he didn't remember. Why would he? I wasn't important to him at that time. "High school? How you bullied me? How I tried so hard and you told me to practice more and when I did, you said I'd never be good enough. That I didn't have the drive to make it in the K-pop world as a dancer. That I . . ." My body trembled. This was so stupid, but it had ruined me for years. Why had I let him ruin me like this?

I stared into his eyes. He merely squatted in front of me, listening. It appeared he didn't remember it at all. Typical.

"Why would you take that to heart?" he finally asked.

"It hurt me. You bullied me. I was never good enough for you."

"I was trying to protect you!"

That caught me off-guard and angered me even more. "Protect me? From what?"

"From the other kids." His voice grew quiet. "Because you were a foreigner."

What? "How did bullying me and stomping on my dream protect me?" I was thoroughly confused.

"I-I thought you knew. I thought if I directed it . . . if I did most of the bullying, then they'd leave you alone."

"Bullshit!" I scooted backwards and lurched to my feet. That wasn't what had happened at all. "That's absolute bullshit! I heard you! I heard you promise them you'd keep me away if they let you into their little clique. You wanted to be popular, and you knew they wouldn't accept you if you were friends with me. You knew that bullying me and pushing me away would guarantee that!"

His mouth fell open. He rose to meet me. "That's . . . that's not true. I never said that." But he had. I remembered it clearly. Me, walking into the gymnasium as he sat with his new friends. He had told them he'd keep me away. And he'd said it with such vehemence that I'd turned right around and skipped gym that day, devastated.

"You did!" I screamed the words. "Get out! I don't want to talk to you anymore!"

"Lindsey—"

"GET OUT!"

Jintae started to say something, changed his mind, turned, and left.

Chapter Fourteen

I did my best to avoid Jintae. If he was home, I stayed in my room or I spent time with Anne or I worked late at the studio.

On Wednesday, Young Sik dropped by my office to show me his album concept. It was a welcome distraction after all the drama with Jintae. *Just one more day,* I told myself. Then he would be gone for three months and I could relax.

Young Sik came into my office with a huge grin on his face. "*Ya,* are you ready for this?"

I stood, smiling, my gaze roaming over his svelte form. Today, he wore a blue and white basketball outfit with a white cap. The sleeveless shirt exposed the sinewy muscles of his arms. And his legs were masses of muscle as well. Goddamn, he was hot! I had to swallow before I drooled all over my desk.

He tossed a jump drive my way and laughed when I fumbled to catch it. I barely managed not to drop it. Sliding it into the USB port of my desktop, I brought up the files and let him take over to show me his masterpiece.

And what a masterpiece it was! The cover used my favorite photo from the shoot. It had the words "I Am Not Your Friend" on it, along with his name. Photos filled the pages of the accompanying booklet from all three shooting locations. He had a full track list of fifteen songs, including the title track.

"I'm sending it off today to get it printed. What do you think?"

"Impressive!" I exclaimed. "I love it. I must buy a copy when it's released."

He waved a hand at me. "I'll give you a copy. It's the least I can do. You made it all possible." Our eyes met, and a heat rushed through me, so powerful I had to avert my gaze, lest I be consumed by the fire. He cleared his throat. "I was wondering if you would like to have lunch with me today? In celebration of a job well-done, of course."

I didn't even have to think about it. "I'd like that," I said, trying to keep my voice steady. Inside, my heart pounded against my chest.

"Sushi?" he asked.

"I love sushi!"

He took me to a little sushi place we had to drive to from my office. I'd never been there, but he insisted they had the best sushi in Korea.

The restaurant was small and cozy. As we slipped into a booth, a server slapped two menus in front of us. She was petite and pretty and gave Young Sik a bright smile.

"Been a while," she said to him. "I was beginning to think you'd forgotten about us."

He gave her a sheepish grin. "Sorry. I've been busy." When I looked at him questioningly, he told me, "This is my cousin, Minhee. Minhee, this is Lindsey. She's the photographer I hired for my new album."

"Nice to meet you," I said, keeping my voice pleasant as I fought to keep that irrational jealousy from sprouting. *She's his cousin,* I reminded myself.

His cousin bowed. "You, too. Wait . . . you're the one from the news, right? Minhyuk's ex?"

I cringed. Oh god. Not this. Not now.

"I'm sorry. I'm totally on your side. I always thought there was something off about him." When I didn't reply, she switched back to server mode. "Anyway, is there anything I can get you to drink while you decide what to eat?"

We ordered colas and she left us.

"Sorry," Young Sik said. "She's a little brazen."

"It's okay." I waved it off and opened the menu. "I know she meant no harm. She just caught me off-guard." I smiled at him. "So, what's good from this place?"

After we ordered, Minhee took our menus and left again, leaving us with cokes and an uncomfortable silence. I sipped my drink, unsure of what to say. I was relieved when Young Sik spoke first.

"Thanks again for the photos. I mean it when I say you did an amazing job."

"My pleasure."

"Oh. I showed the concept to one of my friends. He's going to be releasing a mini album soon. I gave him your number because he was really impressed with your work."

I blushed. "Thank you." While I still thought I wouldn't do many K-pop requests, I found the prospect of another shoot enjoyable.

Young Sik sat back in his seat just as Minhee brought out the sushi.

"So, your friend, Jintae," the rapper said after we were alone again. "You swear he's not your boyfriend?"

I swallowed, nearly choking as a darkness settled over me. "Absolutely not," I swore.

I must have said it with more force than I meant to, for Young Sik held up his hands. "Woah. Did I hit a sore spot? I'm sorry."

"He and I aren't talking right now because he's a selfish asshole."

"I'll admit, he seemed overprotective of you when I was there. Aggressive, even."

I shrugged. I didn't want to talk about Jintae right now. I pushed a piece of sushi around on my plate with my chopsticks.

Young Sik swung his head toward two girls sitting at a table kitty-cornered to us. They had their phones out, blatantly taking photos of him. He frowned, shooting them a glare that made them shrink and hide their phones under their table, lest he smash them. But I also saw something else in their looks. They were afraid, but also in awe of him and probably willing to drop their panties if he asked them.

Goddamn, this guy had the sex appeal of a freaking god.

When he turned back to me, he noticed I had been staring at him the same way the girls had.

"I'd tell you to take a picture, it'll last longer," he said, "but you already took a lot of them."

I couldn't help but laugh. "Around three hundred."

"I'm sorry. About what we were talking about. It obviously makes you uncomfortable to discuss Jintae."

I nodded. "Things happened between us."

"If it's any consolation, talking about him makes me uncomfortable, too."

That squeezed a chuckle from me. I put another piece of sushi in my mouth.

He got quiet, as if he had something to say to me, but was afraid to speak. I looked at him expectantly.

He rubbed the back of his head and took in a sharp breath. "So, um, if you're free on Friday, would you like to go see a movie with me?"

My jaw dropped, and I snapped it closed. I swallowed before answering in a quiet voice, "I-I'm free. I'd love to."

His face lit up. "Great! Is there anything you'd like to see?"

I had no idea what movies were playing, so I shrugged and quipped, "Nothing with Ko Minhyuk in it."

Chapter Fifteen

hen I came home from work that night, Jintae was already there. Upon opening the door, I was assaulted with roses and a box of chocolate-dipped strawberries. Jintae peeked at me from behind them. "Do you forgive me?"

I frowned. No *I'm sorry* or *I was wrong*. He just wanted my forgiveness. Making this all about him.

"No," I said. I pushed past him into the hallway, kicking off my shoes as I went.

"Lindsey, come on. I'm leaving tomorrow. I don't want to go with us like this."

I ignored him and continued on, turning the corner and heading into the kitchen to find a quick snack.

"If you're hungry, these strawberries are nice and sweet," he said, coming up behind me.

I swung around, furious. "See? This is your problem, Jintae! You're not taking this seriously. You're not listening to me. This isn't about you and your damned apologies! This is about me and how you made me feel. How you ruined my life. I'm done. I'll house sit for you like I promised, but I'll be gone before you get back."

His expression drooped and his arms fell limp to his sides. The strawberries and flowers tumbled to the floor. "What can I do to make you forgive me?"

"Stop making this about you!" I screamed. I stomped back to my room and slammed the door. My appetite had fled.

I expected him to come after me, but noises of his movements remained in the kitchen where he was probably cleaning up the mess the flowers and fruit had made after he dropped them. His footsteps retreated, and the door to his bedroom click closed.

Sometime later, I turned off the overhead light and crawled between the sheets, leaving on the desk lamp by my bed.

What was I doing? Why was I being like this to him? I accused him of being selfish, but wasn't I being selfish as well?

I shook my head. No. I had a right to feel this way. He hurt me badly back then. So much that I fled to the US and gave up on my dream of dancing. He deserved my wrath.

I never quite fell asleep. I drifted for a while until I heard a light knock on my door. It clicked open. "Lindsey?" What did he want now? "Are you asleep?"

Yes! I wanted to scream at him, but instead, I lay still, pretending to sleep with my back to him. I heard him creep toward me, and I kept my breathing shallow and relaxed.

"Lindsey?" he whispered again. When I didn't answer he gave a little "Ah, *jinjja* . . ." in frustration.

93

I heard him scratch his head and blow out a puff of air. His footsteps receded, but then they came back again, as if he couldn't decide what to do.

The bed dipped. What the hell was he doing? I remained still as he crawled under the blanket beside me. He snaked his arm around my midsection. I held my breath. His hand was warm on my belly through my pajamas. My heart beat faster. Seriously, what was he doing?

He snuggled up to me, his lips brushing the back of my neck. He showered me with feathery kisses. It took all I had not to ruin my ruse and jump up to ask him what he was doing. Instead, I murmured some nonsense and snuggled deeper into my pillow. His other hand dove beneath me to clasp the one on my belly. He made a noise of frustration at the back of his throat and nuzzled me. I answered with a noise of my own.

His right hand, the one attached to the arm beneath me, roamed upwards, sliding beneath my pajama shirt. I took a sharp intake of air as his warm hand touched my bare skin, but I didn't resist as he cupped my naked breast. As he kissed my neck and exposed shoulder, the other hand traveled downwards. A finger slipped beneath the band of my pajama pants to continue its journey south. Electricity danced across my skin as heat and wetness pooled between my thighs. Any thoughts of hating him flew out of my head, chased out by an intense desire to have him touch me lower.

Then the hand receded, and he tugged on my waistband. "These need to go," he murmured in my ear before giving it a nibble that left me breathless.

94

I mumbled an affirmative and shimmied out of my clothes. He followed. I started to ask myself what I was doing but gave up mid-thought and said, "Fuck it." He was leaving tomorrow. I wouldn't see him for three months, so why not?

I settled back onto the pillow, still facing away from him, and moved my hair out of the way to give him access to my neck, shoulders, and back. He took full advantage of this. His hands resumed their positions, one cupping my breast, the other now settled on the skin beneath my belly button, teasing me with its closeness. As he peppered me with kisses, my body awakened into a wonderland of sensations. Electricity arced from his lips down my spine.

He teased my nipple with his right hand while his left continued its journey south. He stopped just above my clit. His teeth nibbled my ear right as he sunk his middle finger into the folds covering my sensitive nub.

His finger swirled around my most sensitive spot, eliciting a gasp from me as he dipped it lower before bringing it back up to swirl again.

He released my breast and used that arm to prop himself up. I turned until I lay on my back, his finger still holding my clit hostage, though now it just rested there.

His lips sought mine. He had the faint taste of strawberries. I drank him in as his tongue plunged into my mouth.

Oh god, why did he have to feel so good? Why did I have to enjoy it so much that everything else, every other emotion except lust, left my mind?

I moaned and tangled my fingers in his messy blonde hair, pulling him closer. His marshmallow lips melded with mine.

His hand left my clit, and he swung himself over me, bracing himself on his hands. I opened my legs wide, and he settled between them, nestling his hard phallus within my folds, but not quite entering me.

Our eyes met. I wanted to avoid his, but they captured me, the slits curving as he smiled. I stared at him, my mouth slightly agape. He brushed a few wayward strands of hair from my face.

"I need you," he whispered. And I needed him, too. I wrapped my legs around him, but I didn't speak. I couldn't. My mind refused to let me say anything.

He thrust into me, filling me and groaning as our hips met. "Oh god, you feel so good," he murmured, pulling out a little only to drive himself inside even harder. "Fuck, Lindsey, do you know what you do to me?"

I knew, but I remained quiet. I lay still as he pulled out, slowly this time. He watched himself as he did so. His hair hung in front of his face, obscuring his eyes, but I still saw his pink lips, which parted as he pushed himself into my heat. Oh god. I grabbed his ass and pulled him into me as deep as I could. My eyes closed and my head fell back.

His lips sought the delicate underside of my throat., right beneath my chin. He thrust into me with each kiss, now seeking my lips. Redistributing his weight to his left arm, he palmed the back of my head with his right hand, groaning into my mouth as his fingers twisted themselves in my hair.

I wasn't expecting to orgasm so fast—after all, who orgasms with someone they hate?—but my clit blossomed at the touch of his groin hitting it. My fingers dug into the flesh of his ass like claws, pulling him into me again and again, our bodies slamming together until the sweet release rolled over me in waves. I gasped and panted and switched my arms so I clung to him, wrapping myself around his upper torso.

His breathing grew ragged, his thrusts erratic, faster and faster until he buried his face in my hair and cried out as he filled me with his cum, his body stiff as he released inside me.

He relaxed, and, after a minute, he pulled out and lay beside me. I snuggled my backside against him. He threw an arm over me, clutching me to him like he never wanted to let me go.

And we fell asleep.

Chapter Sixteen

I awoke to soft kisses butterflying my cheek, by my ear, across my forehead.

When my eyes fluttered open, Jintae was smiling at me. He brushed my hair aside and nuzzled my ear.

"Do you forgive me now?" he asked. His voice was soft, but it scraped across my last nerve. How dare he? How dare he ask that of all things, after what we had together last night?

My temper flared, and I jerked away from him, bolting upright and glaring at him. "Is that all you care about? Getting me to forgive you?"

His mouth popped open, confusion on his face. "Lindsey, I—"

"Don't you 'Lindsey' me!" I growled at him. "I told you. This isn't about you. This isn't about forgiveness. You hurt me back then. You ruined me!" Tears blinked from my eyes.

"I don't know what you want me to say," he whimpered, drawing back.

I huffed. "I don't want you to *say* anything. I want you to understand. I want you to understand what you did to me. How I felt."

When he just sat there with that stupid, little, cute look of confusion on his face, I surged out of bed. "You know what . . . fine. Whatever. I'm done. Done with this. Done with you. Enjoy your trip. I'll be gone before you get back." And with that, I flounced naked from the room, making my way to the half-bath to brush my teeth and throw on a robe I'd hung in there.

He came knocking, and I refused to open the door for him. "Go away," I said. "Go on your tour. Leave me alone."

"Lindsey," he said. "Help me understand. I don't understand what I did wrong."

"Go away!" I wanted him gone. I didn't want to talk to him anymore. I didn't want to see him. I didn't want to be distracted again by those goddamned marshmallow lips or those carved, sexy eyes. I wanted him to go.

I knew if I waited long enough, he'd have to leave. And sure enough, he did. His phone rang. I heard him answer it and say, "I'll be right down" in a reluctant voice. Then he tapped on the bathroom door and said, "I have to go. Please open the door." His words sounded like they were spoken through tears. He was losing me and he knew it.

I still refused to open the door, to speak to him, practically holding my breath until he left, the front door slamming behind him.

And still I sat on the toilet with the lid down, waiting and counting the seconds until I was certain he was gone, before opening the door and creeping out and into the kitchen. The apartment had an eerie silence to it.

I almost expected Jintae to come out from his bedroom and tackle me in a hug—almost relished the thought, even—but he was truly gone.

Chapter Seventeen

Jintae sent me a few texts early in the day, to which I replied in as few words as possible, ignoring any pleas to discuss what had gone on between us.

Then Friday rolled around, and I thought of Young Sik instead. He deserved my attention more than Jintae, for he had never hurt me, and he was sweet and kind and I enjoyed being with him.

He called me around three pm to make sure we were still on for the movie and, when I said yes, he told me he'd pick me up around seven-thirty for the eight o'clock showing of a popular Korean movie that was taking the world by storm. I had been wanting to see it, and so had he.

I told him I'd wait out front, since I meant to keep my word to Jintae about no strange men in the house, even if we weren't on the best of terms right now. Part of me hoped Jintae would come around and see the error of his ways. The other part was excited to be spending an evening with Young Sik.

I dressed for our date in an emerald green, scoop-necked t-shirt and a black pencil skirt. I hated heels, so I wore a pair of cute black clogs. I had pulled my hair back in a ponytail, and I wore a black baseball cap. While waiting out front, I fiddled with a black face mask. I'd wear it when we checked in at the theater. With our popularity, it was a must.

Young Sik pulled up in a sleek, black sports car a few minutes after I stepped outside. When I'd asked him what to look for, he'd told me he didn't splurge much, but this car was his pride and joy, a symbol he'd finally made it.

He stepped out of the car and skirted around the hood to open my door, and I swear my panties were wet right then. Oh god, he was sexy. Tall, with his dark hair slicked back, a small gold hoop dangling from his left ear. He wore blue jeans and a white collared shirt with a tan suede jacket and boots to match. Rings adorned his fingers, thick bands in silver and black.

He grinned at me. "Ready?" he asked, his eyes sweeping the length of me.

I swallowed and nodded. When his hand touched the small of my back to guide me into his car, electricity raced along my spine.

"You look beautiful," he said before closing the door. I bet my face was as red as my hair at his words.

We put on our masks before getting out of the car at the theater and took them off again once we settled in our seats. He had also donned a cap once we arrived. I left my hat on, but Young Sik set his next to him after the lights shut off and the screen lit up.

The movie was as good as the critics had said it would be. About halfway through, we ran out of popcorn and Young Sik reached over and took my hand in his, bringing it to his lips. I turned my head to watch him, electricity zipping from my heart straight to my loins as his lips feathered against the back of my hand. Then he settled it in his lap and focused on the movie. The heat from his hand added to the anticipation I was feeling. Where was this going to lead?

Afterward, we strolled back toward the car, incognito and hand-in-hand, discussing how great the movie was.

I leaned against the car as he opened the door for me, but instead of guiding me inside, he pulled his mask below his chin and brought his face close to mine. I removed my mask, my heart pounding in my chest.

After we'd finished the popcorn in the theater, he'd pulled out a chocolate bar while I'd enjoyed some cherry licorice twists. The faint scent of chocolate now wafted over me as he drew closer. He turned his hat backwards.

My eyes fluttered closed as he brushed his lips against mine. They were thinner than Jintae's but no less luscious. He brought his hand up to caress my cheek as he deepened the kiss. My mouth filled with the taste of chocolate. I melted into him.

When he drew back, his eyes flashed with mischief. "So, shall I drop you off at your place . . . or would you like to visit mine for a bit?"

"Your place sounds nice," I breathed, and I allowed him to guide me into my seat. Gods, his kiss left my knees weak!

When we arrived at his apartment, Young Sik apologized in advance for the state it was in, though the neighborhood appeared peaceful. "I'd rather put my money into my music," he said.

"And your car," I replied with a smirk.

He gave a sheepish grin. "My one luxury."

"Nothing wrong with that. Sometimes I cringe at the ungodly amount I've spent on camera equipment. Especially my lenses." But thinking of those brought a pang to my heart. Minhyuk still had most my personal lenses, including a nine million won telephoto lens I'd bought only a month ago.

"You okay?"

I put on a brave smile. "Yeah."

I followed him to his apartment on the ground level, accessible via a low-walled walkway. Unlike Jintae's condo, there were no security measures beyond a security pad on Young Sik's door.

He punched in the code. The door clicked, and he opened it, drawing me inside.

His lips met mine before I even thought about taking off my shoes. He backed me against the door, pressing his hardness into me as our tongues danced. The taste of him was still chocolate, and it drove me wild.

He knocked the hat from my head and pulled the band from my hair, leaving it to cascade around my face and shoulders.

"I want all of you," he breathed before assaulting me with kisses.

And then my phone rang.

104

"Just a minute," I said, meaning to turn it off, but when I saw the caller ID, I rolled my eyes. "Sorry. I need to take this."

I'd promised Jintae I'd answer whenever he called because it might be important.

Jintae didn't even give me the chance to say hello. "Where are you? Are you home?"

"I'm out. Why?" My gaze roamed to Young Sik, who watched me with a slight puzzlement on his face. I offered him a silent apology.

"The motion sensor went off on the balcony. Hopefully, it's just a cat or something, but I need you to check to be sure."

"Did the camera pick up anything?"

"No. Something's blocking it. Looks like a spiderweb, maybe. I just need you to look into it, okay? Where are you, anyway? Working?"

"I said I'm out." I couldn't hide the irritation in my voice. It wasn't any of his business where I was.

At that moment, Young Sik cleared his throat—rather loudly—the bastard.

"Are you with someone?"

I shot daggers Young Sik's way before replying, "I'm with Young Sik, okay? Is that a problem?"

"Err . . ." Jintae fell silent for a moment, then, "I guess not." But I could sense hurt in his words. A tiny pang of guilt hit me.

"I'll go check it out," I said, not unkindly. "I was heading home anyway." The lie rolled off my tongue.

"Call me when you get there. And, um, take Young Sik with you in case it isn't a cat."

105

"Okay. I will," I said, feeling even more guilty now.

Young Sik had no issue driving me back to check on the condo. When we got there, I punched in the code and opened the door.

The condo was dark and quiet by the foyer, but I saw lighting coming from deeper within. I wasn't sure if I'd left any lights on, so I trudged down the hallway with little thought to any dangers that might be lurking. Young Sik followed.

As I rounded the corner, something hit me hard, knocking me into the wall by Jintae's bedroom door. The air in my lungs left me in a rush as someone shoved me into the wall.

I saw a glint of steel a split second before the intruder was pulled off me. A brief struggle ensued, resulting in the person rushing past me and out the door.

Gentle hands helped me stand. "Are you okay?" Young Sik asked. I leaned against him, my knees weak and my heart hammering in my chest.

"I think so," I whispered. It had happened so fast, my brain was still trying to process what had happened. "Is he gone?"

"Yeah. Come on, let's get you to the couch."

Young Sik ended up carrying me as I couldn't get my legs to work. After setting me down, he asked where the light switch was. I pointed in its general direction. As I did so, I noticed the ambient light in the otherwise dark condo was coming from my bedroom.

I distinctly remembered turned that light off before leaving.

"Young Sik," I said. He turned toward me and I pointed. "He was in my bedroom. The light." I rose unsteadily from the couch, and Young Sik rushed back over to help me. I pushed him away. "I'm fine." And I started for my room.

"Lindsey, wait!" he called and grabbed my elbow. "Let me go first. There might be another." He looked toward the balcony. I followed his gaze. The curtains covering the sliding glass door fluttered as a breeze blew through. "Just a minute." He stalked over to the door. Brushing the curtains aside, we saw it stood open. "No visible damage. It was probably lock-picked."

He started to put his hand on it to close it, but I stopped him. "We need to call the police. Try not to touch anything."

"Oh, right."

We continued to the bedroom. I let Young Sik go first. When he told me all was clear, I entered. My gaze was drawn to a pillowcase sitting on my bed. A pillowcase I most definitely had not put there. A pillowcase I recognized as coming from Minhyuk's place, black with a pattern of blue triangles. I'd laid my head to rest on a similar one over the past two years. This one was filled with objects made up of sharp angles and round parts.

Young Sik noticed it, too, and tilted his head. "What is that?" he asked, as a gasp of recognition escaped me.

I knew exactly what it was.

"Oh no!" I ripped open the pillowcase, my heart plummeting to my feet. Inside were my lenses. They'd been shattered into dozens of pieces.

Chapter Eighteen

Young Sik called the police while I sat on the bed, my head in my hands. Over a dozen lenses—twenty million won worth of equipment—were ruined. And why were they here? What had Minhyuk planned with this?

A pair of police officers showed up several minutes later. By then, I had moved back out to the couch and sat there nursing a mug of Sleepy Time tea that Young Sik insisted on making me. I hadn't called Jintae yet, though I intended to do so after the cops left. Truth is, I was dreading making that call.

"It's strange," I heard one officer tell Young Sik. "About an hour ago, we got a call from Ko Minhyuk alleging someone broke into his home."

I perked up at that. What? "Minhyuk reported a break-in?"

"Yes," the officer said. "He said all that was stolen were your things, and he alleged you had sent a thief to get them back."

Young Sik and I exchanged glances. Standing beside the officer, he said, "But if that were true, why are her lenses broken? And why was the condo broken into?"

The officer shrugged. "He didn't mention their condition."

By now I was fuming. "He tried to set me up, didn't he? Oh my god, Young Sik!" Angry tears spilled from my eyes and the rapper came over to gather me into an embrace.

The police dusted for fingerprints, but the intruder had been wearing gloves, so there was nothing to lift.

The spiderweb Jintae had said was covering his motion camera turned out to be a light spray of white paint. The intruder must have sprayed it before setting off the motion detector.

Young Sik promised me he'd help find a better setup on Monday so this wouldn't happen again.

After the police left, I sat on the couch in a daze. My tea has gone cold, so Young Sik was busy making a fresh cup when I remembered I needed to call Jintae.

He picked up right away. "Lindsey? Are you okay? What took so long? Is everything all right?"

I took in a deep, shuddering breath. "There was someone here," I said, my voice barely above a whisper. And then I broke down crying.

It took a while for him to get the entire story as everything came crashing upon me. Young Sik rushed over with the tea and put an arm around me, crushing me to his chest as I sobbed into the phone. He took the phone from me and explained what had happened.

"I'll take care of her," he promised. "Don't worry . . . yeah. I'll stay as long as she needs me."

After he hung up, he put both arms around me. "It'll be okay. I won't let anything happen to you."

Sometime later, I awoke in my bed, not sure how I got there. My memory was hazy after the phone call, and I guessed I must have passed out in Young Sik's arms.

Early daylight streamed in the window, so I'd slept all night. I sat up and went to reach for my phone. It sat on my bedside table. Only Young Sik could have put it there, on the charger, even.

Speaking of Young Sik, he lay asleep on the floor, cocooned in blankets from Jintae's bed. I wondered what Jintae would think of him going into his room and decided he must never know.

Young Sik looked peaceful with his arms wrapped around the pillow his head rested on as he lay on his stomach. I didn't want to disturb him, so I padded to my dresser to grab some clothes. I let myself out of the room and made for the shower in Jintae's room, stopping by the half bath to grab my toothbrush and toothpaste.

After I was showered and feeling human again, I returned to my bedroom, dressed in a t-shirt and yoga pants, to find Young Sik sitting up and stretching.

He saw me and smiled, rubbing the sleep from one eye with his fist. His normally slicked back hair was tousled and tangled from sleeping.

"You're up?" he asked and unwound himself from the blankets. He wore his shirt and boxers. His jeans were pooled on the floor beside him.

I turned my head as he dressed. "Yeah. I didn't mean to wake you, but I *really* needed a shower."

"Mm. Me too. If you think you'll be okay, I'd like to hop back to my apartment and do that, plus pack some things so I can stay with you for a few days . . . if that's all right?"

I turned back to find him straightening his shirt over his jeans. "That would be great. I'd appreciate it."

He grinned. God, he looked irresistible with his hair mussed like that. "I'll bring back breakfast. I saw a waffle place not too far from here."

"Oh! Yes! They have wonderful food. Their apple waffles are delicious. Plus, their whipped cream is amazing."

"Apple waffles it is," he replied.

After Young Sik left, I sat on my bed, going through my lenses and getting angrier with each broken one. None of them had survived. In a fury, I picked up my phone and dialed Minhyuk's number. I knew this would be a mistake, but I did it anyway.

I'll be honest. I wasn't expecting him to pick up, so it surprised me when he answered on the second ring.

He didn't waste any time either. "I knew you'd be calling me," he said instead of a greeting. "Did you get your lenses back?"

"Fuck you," I replied. "Yes. I got them back. All broken. What the fuck, Minhyuk? That was twenty million won worth of equipment you destroyed. I didn't even—" I stopped as a

111

lump rose in my throat. I tried to keep my cool, but I was failing miserably. Tears welled in my eyes. "I didn't even get to use my sixteen-hundred millimeter, you fucking asshole." The phone trembled in my grasp. When he didn't reply, I continued. "Why are you doing this, huh? What did I ever do to you? Goddammit, Minhyuk, I *loved* you!" Angry tears seared my cheeks. "Why did you do this? Why?"

Still nothing but silence on the other end. I thought he'd broken the connection until I heard him exhale. "Lindsey," he said, his voice not unkind. "Don't cry."

"She did it, didn't she?"

"I'm sorry," he said. "I-I'll wire you some money."

He hung up before I could say anything more.

I dropped my hand to my lap, feeling . . . strange. Like I seriously didn't know how to feel right now. He denied nothing. He didn't fight me on it, either.

I heard the front door open, and I wandered out of the room. Young Sik came around the corner with a large paper bag in one hand and his suitcase in the other.

"I got breakfast!" He grinned at me, but his face fell when he saw the look on mine. "Are you okay?"

I nodded and wiped at my tears, forcing myself to smile. "Yeah. Just a little confused." I told him about the phone call with Minhyuk.

We met at the table, and he unpacked the bag, setting things out between us as I talked.

"Damn, that's strange," he said. "Almost like he's actually sorry for what he did . . . or she did, if you believe him."

"It's a complete turnaround. I don't know how to take it." We sat, and I took the cover off my waffles. The apple cinnamon scent made my mouth water.

"I wouldn't worry about it for now," Young Sik said. He opened his container to reveal chocolate chip waffles drizzled with a rich chocolate syrup. "Wait and see if he sends you the money. It's strange, though. Last night he sent someone to break in and deposit your broken lenses on your bed, yet this morning he's promising to pay for them? I wouldn't trust him."

"Hmm, you're right. I really shouldn't trust him." I scooped the whipped cream from its container and dropped it onto my waffles. This whipped cream was as thick as butter and some of the best tasting cream I've ever had. I licked the fork clean and used it to cut my waffle, then I took a bite. Absolute heaven.

Young Sik must have felt the same, for he began stuffing his face, groaning with every bite.

After we were done, I rinsed the plastic containers in the sink and set them to dry.

Arms encircled me. The scent of chocolate filled my nostrils as Young Sik's voice tickled my right ear. "Shall we pick up where we left off last night?" he asked. His tongue glided along my earlobe, sending shivers down my spine.

I turned and draped my arms over his shoulders. When I tilted my head toward him, he met me, covering my mouth with his. Chocolate rolled over my taste buds as his tongue explored my mouth. He lifted me onto the counter. My legs wrapped themselves around his waist. We only broke the kiss to pull each other's shirts over our heads. He trailed kisses down to my bra and released it with a snap of his fingers. His mouth sought a nipple, pulling it within as he sucked on it, his tongue dancing around the sensitive flesh. I let out a quiet moan. Lightning danced along my spine, heating my core.

He slid his right hand up my thigh and tugged on the waistband of my yoga pants. I lifted my butt off the counter so he could pull them down and off me, revealing black satin panties. I let out a gasp as he slipped one of his fingers under the satin to slide through my wet folds.

Young Sik growled and moved up to nibble on my neck. "I want you right now." He thrust himself against me, the hardness beneath his jeans giving me warning of what was to come.

"Then take me," I said, lifting my ass again as he shimmied my panties off me. He unbuckled his jeans, and they dropped to the floor, revealing boxer briefs and a large bulge.

I couldn't help it. My eyes widened as he pulled the boxers down and his dick sprang free. It was as long and lanky as he was. I'll admit, I wasn't expecting that.

He laughed, noticing my look. "I'm a bit large."

"A bit?" I gave his dick a nervous glance.

"If it's intimidating, we don't have to."

"No. No, I'm game," I said, swallowing.

"I'll be slow and careful. If it hurts, tell me. I'll be honest, I haven't met a woman who can take it all, so I won't be upset or anything."

Well, hell. Challenge accepted. I was determined to be the first.

114

I have to admit, fear sparked within me as he ran the tip of his cock through my folds. I was more than ready for him, but could I take it all?

He caught my mouth with his, one hand on the back of my head, the other guiding himself inside me. Oh god. I shuddered as he slid through my hot, wet flesh. Sitting on the counter put me at the optimal height for him. He pushed himself deeper, groaning into my mouth and flooding my taste buds with more of that delicious chocolate flavor.

My pussy eagerly devoured him. It quivered as he rocked back and forth, in and out, sinking a little deeper with each new thrust. I wanted it. I wanted it all, and I couldn't stand it any longer. I grabbed his hips and thrust myself against him until I buried him to the hilt. It hurt. Oh god, did it hurt! But it also made my nerves come alive with pleasure. He stopped kissing me and hooked his chin over my shoulder, groaning even louder. His hands went to my hips, and he pulled me toward him until our hipbones touched.

"Are you okay?" he asked. "Does it hurt?"

"It hurts good," I breathed. "Don't stop."

He started moving again, sending delicious shocks through me. I'd never felt anything like it. I gripped his ass, forcing him into me again and again.

"Fuck. I'm not going to last long," he said into my hair. He stilled and brushed my clit with his thumb. I jerked against it, wanting him to touch me there. My pussy pulsed, already milking him as he rubbed. He shoved into me again and everything released, the orgasm washing over me. I shuddered around him, clenching him hard inside me. He cried out, "Oh fuck, baby," and slammed into me, harder and harder. With a final thrust, he growled, his teeth nipping at the skin on my shoulder as he came inside me. "Oh fuck. That was amazing," he breathed into my ear. He pulled out of me and pressed his forehead to mine.

We stayed that way until our breathing slowed. Sweat dripped from the tip of his nose. I had my fingers entwined behind his neck. He planted a gentle kiss on my lips. "Are you okay?" he asked. "Did I hurt you?"

I smiled at him. "I'm okay."

He took a step back and helped me off the counter. My legs were wobblier than I thought, and I fell against his bare chest.

"You sure you're okay?"

"I'll be fine." I straightened, and my womb protested. He really did have a deep reach.

"You didn't have to take it all, you know." Was he chastising me?

I smirked. "I know. I couldn't help it. I needed all of you."

We dressed, but only partly, for he suggested we take a shower together.

Jintae probably would have been mad if he found out a "strange man" was using his shower, but what Jintae didn't know wouldn't hurt him.

Young Sik grabbed his bathing supplies from his suitcase while I got the water ready.

I stepped under the warm stream. The heat loosened the knots of pain in my belly. He joined me a minute later and offered to wash and condition my hair. His fingers felt divine on my scalp. I wanted to return the favor, and he got on his knees so I could do the same.

After he rinsed, he turned to face me, still on his knees. His cheek rested on my belly, and he wrapped his arms around my thighs.

"*Johahaeyo,*" he whispered.

I froze. He—he liked me?

He looked up at me, searching my face, seeing something there that concerned him. "Is it too soon? I'm sorry. I can't help it. I like you, Lindsey. I like you a lot."

The water splashed down on us in an invigorating rain.

"I like you, too," I said.

Chapter Nineteen

While I worked on Monday, Young Sik took time from his schedule to purchase and install a new motion camera on Jintae's balcony. He also replaced the lock with a sturdier one. Everything was up and running by the time I came home around five.

"Did you go to the studio today?" I asked him as he set up an app for the camera on my phone.

"No. I took the day off. I'll go back tomorrow. I wanted to make sure you'd be safe."

I sent Jintae a text with a link to the new camera app and the info he'd need to access it. His earlier messages caught my eye. He hadn't had time to call me, but he'd sent a quick text each night to make sure I was okay. Young Sik was going home today, so Jintae promised he'd call as soon as he had a free moment.

I would miss Young Sik's presence, but he had things to do at home and we felt confident that the danger was over. Yesterday, we'd spent the entire day cuddling. I was too sore for sex and he'd chastised me again. To which I told him I'd do it all over again. I just needed time to get used to him. He promised I'd have plenty of time for that.

Monday night, I got a call from Jintae.

"I don't have long," he said. "I just wanted to make sure you were okay."

"I'm fine, thanks," I replied. "Did you get the app set up for the camera?"

"I did. I love it. You guys made a good choice. I'll pay you back when I get home."

"I had nothing to do with it. It was all Young Sik."

"Well, thank him for me then."

I laughed. "I will. How's the tour going?"

"Woah. Asking about me? Does this mean you forgive me?"

I sighed. This again? "Jintae, once again, you are asking the wrong question." I kept my voice calm, civil.

"Then what question should I be asking? I don't understand."

"I told you already. Maybe think about how your actions affected me." I felt like a teacher trying to nudge a little boy in the right direction.

"I—hold on a minute." I heard him cover the phone and his muffled voice called out, "I'll be right there!" He came back on the line. "I'll think about it. I gotta go. The next few weeks are going to be busy, so I may not call much, but I'll try to text you every day. Stay safe, love." And with that, he ended the call.

Chapter Twenty

Unexpectedly, the first month of Jintae's world tour flew by. The three of us were busier than we expected to be. Jintae with his tour, me with my photography (which was even more popular than ever. I landed two big drama deals), and Young Sik with his album release and several music videos.

To my surprise, Minhyuk kept his word, and I received money to replace most of the broken lenses.

Young Sik and I still found time to see each other. And we grew closer. The sex was amazing and my body adapted to his size, thank goodness! He always smelled and tasted like chocolate, something that made my mouth water and left me craving more.

I didn't hear much from Jintae because of his busy schedule, but he made a point to send me a brief text whenever he could.

And then, a month and a half into his tour, he found the time to call me.

I had just stepped out of the shower after a long day at work with plans to cook *ramyeon* and hit the bed when I got a text from him.

I have time tonight. How about a video call? I have something important to say.

I replied, *A video call? I'm not exactly decent. I just got out of the shower.*

Jintae sent a sticker of a rabbit throwing hearts. *Even better!*

I scoffed and replied, *Fine. Just give me 2 minutes.* I hurried to throw on my jammies.

When he called, I was relaxing on the couch, hoping I didn't look *too* relaxed. His beautiful face appeared on my screen. He broke into a grin when he saw me. "God, I missed your face."

"Are you buttering me up for something?" I asked, but I smiled, too.

"Me?" He raised his perfectly plucked eyebrows. "You accuse *me*?" He had laughter in his eyes. "Okay. So maybe I am. Actually, I wanted to tell you I think I know what you want me to say to you."

I sat up. "You do?"

He nodded and grew serious. "Lindsey, I'm sorry." His image grew bouncy as he moved the phone, placing it somewhere so I could see all of him. He got on his knees. "I'm sorry I hurt you back then. I'm sorry for being selfish. I know I don't deserve your forgiveness. What I said back then . . . part of me thought I was helping you by pushing you away, by teasing you, and by telling you you'd never be good enough to be a dancer. But most of me was selfish. I wanted to fit in with the popular kids, and I used you to do that." He looked away, no longer able to meet my gaze. "I hurt you, and I ruined you, and I was so selfish that I didn't realize what my actions had done to you. How they'd affected you until it was too late and you were gone."

He sniffled. My god, Jintae was . . . crying. My heart wrenched in my chest. His eyes lifted to meet mine again. I almost forgot we were separated by thousands of miles. Tears glistened on his cheeks and red limned his perfectly carved eyelids. "I am so sorry," he said. "I never meant . . . no, I never thought I'd lose you like that. I loved you so much, even back then, and I was foolishly confident that you'd always be there. That you'd always love me. I know you tried so hard, and you always listened to anything I said." He exhaled a long, sad breath of air. "When I had to go back to Korea early for the operation, I took comfort in the fact that we'd soon be reunited. And then I fucked it all up by being stupid and selfish. I hurt you so much and yet, you still tried so hard to please me.

"Lindsey, I know I don't deserve forgiveness. I know I can't go back and make everything right again. All I can do is try hard to make sure no one—not me, not Young Sik or Minhyuk—*no one* hurts you again. I'm sorry, baby. I'm so, so sorry."

As he spoke, a lump formed in my throat. He got it. He really got it. I blinked away tears and tried to swallow the lump. "Jintae," I breathed. "Thank you." The tears fell anyway, and I wiped them away.

"I wish I were there to hold you," he said. He grabbed the phone and brought it so his entire face filled the screen. "I miss you, baby."

I smiled. "I miss you, too. I . . . Jintae, I have to tell you something about back then, too. I never hated you. The whole time, I thought it was me. I thought I was the problem, and I just needed to try harder. And when that didn't work, I truly thought I wasn't good enough. I believed you. I believed I was a failure. I left because I couldn't face you anymore. I thought it might be better if I were out of your life. I blamed myself for everything. And I gave up on everything."

He winced. "Oh, baby, I'm sorry. I'm so sorry. I didn't know. I really didn't. I was too stuck on myself. *Aigoo,* I just want to give you a hug right now."

We fell silent, neither of us knowing what to say after this. He stared at me with concern on his face. I stared back, my cheeks hot with tears.

"Lindsey," he finally said, his voice hoarse with emotion. He cleared his throat. "I don't want you to leave. I want you to stay with me. You haven't found a place, right?"

"I've barely started to look," I admitted.

"Just stay. I want you there when I get back. I want you in my bed every night. You're the only way I can sleep. All these years, I've spent my nights tossing and turning, but with you beside me I can sleep again. I—I love you so much, baby, that it hurts. I know I don't deserve you, but I need you."

I didn't know how to answer that. His selfishness was showing again, but for some reason, in this context, I didn't mind. He *needed* me.

But what about Young Sik? God, I liked him so much. He was a joy to be with, and I could see myself spending the rest of my life with him.

"Why aren't you saying anything?" Jintae's voice snapped me back. I focused on his image to see him frowning. "You're thinking about *him,* aren't you?"

I wasn't going to lie. "I am."

His features eased. "He's a good man. As much as I hate to admit it, he is. And he's never hurt you. Not like I did." He scrubbed his face with his free hand. "You can still stay, Lindsey. You're my best friend. You always have been. Just . . . maybe just give me a chance when you get back." I nodded, and he said, "I gotta go. I'll call you again tomorrow if that's all right."

"Of course it is," I said. Then, "Jintae . . . I love you."

Chapter Twenty-One

Surprisingly, the rest of Jintae's tour passed in a blur. Young Sik's album released to critical acclaim. Even Jintae admitted it was well-done. My list of photography clients continued to grow, and I officially added "K-pop Albums" to my list of services. I was also able to hire additional employees to help.

I grew closer to both guys. The rift between Jintae and me had healed, and I couldn't help but love him as much as before.

I didn't know what to tell Young Sik. He didn't know about the conversation I'd had mending things with Jintae, and I was afraid to tell him. I didn't want to lose him.

Now who was the selfish one?

A week before Jintae was due home, I came clean with Young Sik. I cared too much about him to keep him in the dark any longer.

We sat on the couch at his place watching a drama on tv. He had his arm draped around my shoulders and was teasing my right boob with his long, delicate fingers. It tickled and I slapped playfully at him before mashing his fingers against me with my hand.

"Young Sik," I said as the drama ended. "We need to talk. I have something to tell you."

He took his arm back and faced me. He paled as he asked, "Is it something bad?"

I shrugged and fiddled with the bottom of my shirt.

He cocked his head. "Is it about Jintae coming back next week?"

I nodded, still unable to look him in the eye. Tears welled.

"You talked to him and he made things right, didn't he?"

I blinked and jerked my head his way. "How did you know?"

He lifted a shoulder. "What else could it be? So he apologized. Are you going to try and make things work with him?"

I averted my gaze. "I dunno."

"Lindsey, don't feel bad about what you want to do. It's your choice to make. I won't be angry."

It was then that I fell in love with Young Sik. Goddammit. He was so selfless my heart hurt.

"I feel so selfish," I whispered.

"You're not being selfish. You need to be happy. You *deserve* to be happy. You've known Jintae a lot longer than you've known me. I understand."

"I wish I could be with both of you," I said. Shit. What was I saying? This was madness.

He surprised me. "I wouldn't be opposed to that," he said with a shrug.

126

My eyes widened. "Young Sik!"

"What? I'm not opposed to sharing. It could be . . . fun."
He touched my cheek with a finger.

I grew hot under his touch. He leaned forward and brushed
his lips against mine. Tangling his fingers in my hair, he
brought me closer, deepening the kiss.

"Think about it," he murmured in my ear. "One of us
kissing you while the other pounds that sweet pussy of yours.
Mmm."

My muscles clenched at the thought, bringing forth a gush
of wetness between my thighs. Oh. My. God. This guy. I
groaned into his mouth.

"You know. Jintae is hot. Just imagine all the things we
could do as a threesome."

Jintae is . . .? "Young Sik, are you—?"

"Bi," he replied. "I'm bisexual."

Why did that confession turn me on so much? "Oh god.
Just fuck me now."

"With pleasure," he breathed. "Let's go to my bedroom,
neh?"

Without warning, he scooped me up into his arms. I
squealed and latched around his neck. His eyes met mine and
fire flared through my body. We stayed that way for a few
precious seconds until I hid my face against his shoulder to
hide my tears. God, I loved this man. I loved him and I wanted
him to be mine. Being in a relationship with him and Jintae
was out of the question. But, damn, I wanted that. I wanted it
so much right now.

"We still have a week," he whispered in my ear, "and I plan on making good use of it."

I peeked at him. He was so casual about this. Like it was fine no matter what happened. He was one to go with the flow and not worry about where it would lead him. Wherever he ended up, he'd just shrug and keep going.

Young Sik pushed open the door to his tiny bedroom and placed me on the bed. There was barely enough room to stand in the room with his dresser and a desk. The easiest way to access the bed was crawling up from the foot of it.

I scooted until I lay amongst the pillows and undressed as he did the same.

Naked, he crawled onto the bed and stalked toward me, the evil grin on his face making me shudder like I was being watched by a predator. I splayed my legs, and he crawled between them, gliding his hand along my thigh as he moved.

"So smooth," he noted. His gaze flicked to mine. "Whatever shall I do with you?"

The look in his eye sent a shiver along my spine. He looked dangerous, like in one of his music videos. I swallowed and stuttered, "Whatever you want." He wouldn't hurt me, but just the thought of his hands roughly on me gave me a thrill.

He kneeled between my legs, looking me up and down. "Goddamn, you're gorgeous, Lindsey." His long member throbbed as he spoke. His head dipped forward, and he planted a kiss at the apex of my pussy, right above my clit. His fingers followed, touching the sensitive flesh around my nether lips. "Is your hair down here as red as your hair?"

Since I shaved there, he wouldn't know. "It's darker," I managed to say as he touched his tongue to my nub.

He slipped his hands beneath my ass and lifted me up to feast. Oh god, he worked magic with his tongue! Each swipe and swirl made me quiver as the heat grew within me.

When I grabbed his head to push his face into me, he drew back. "Not yet," he said. "You don't get to come yet."

I whimpered, but he gave me a lopsided grin. He glided up my body until he hovered over me. When he kissed me, I tasted sex and chocolate on his lips.

He positioned himself at my entrance and pushed inside me, inch by inch. My muscles clenched around him, coaxing a moan from the back of his throat.

"Oh god, what you do to me," he whispered, and he plunged his tongue into my mouth once more.

He worked me slowly, in and out, and my pussy gripped him. I wanted to come so badly—I was so close—but every time I slid my hand to my clit, he'd bat it away, saying, "Not yet."

"Young Sik," I protested. "I need to come!"

"Not yet," he said again and drew his dick out only to ram it hard back inside me. Lightning exploded through my belly. He did this a few times, then moved to angle himself differently, and now his length slid along my clit as he plunged inside me again and again.

The sensation drove me crazy. I bucked my hips to keep him in contact as much as possible. My fingers dug into the cheeks of his ass as I moved to keep us close.

When the orgasm burst inside me, my muscles clenched him so hard, he shouted out, "Fuck!" His thrusting became erratic, and he pumped faster until he exploded deep within me.

His body collapsed against mine. "Oh, fuck, Lindsey, what have you done to me? My god, that was amazing."

I wrapped my arms around him, the hearts of our sweating bodies beating in unison. "What did *you* do to *me?*" I asked him. "I've never come so hard in my life."

"I know. I felt it." He lifted himself up and pulled out, rolling onto his back beside me as I let go of him. He lay with his hands on his forehead, elbows in the air, slicking his hair back, still panting.

"Fuck," he said. "I'm a fool to give this up." He turned his head to stare at me. "I don't want to give you up."

My heart wrenched. How could I respond to that? He rolled back on top of me.

"I think I love you," he said.

Chapter Twenty-Two

On the day Jintae was due to return, I made my sure my calendar was clear of clients. He'd texted me that morning to tell me he expected to arrive at the airport around noon, but it would be a few hours before he came home. First, he had to stop by his agency and help unload the equipment.

Around three, I started making him a special meal. I couldn't believe how excited I was to see him again. So excited that I trembled as I mixed and cooked. Ever since he'd apologized to me, we'd become closer. He went from texting me most nights to calling or video chatting. The love that I'd had for him so many years ago grew and bloomed into something wonderful.

But as I cooked, my thoughts wandered to Young Sik and his confession of love. It hurt my heart. I'd played him, even though he insisted he was well aware of my situation and how things would end.

I hadn't seen him since that night. If I called him, he claimed to be busy and promised to meet with me later, but that never happened. Guilt flooded me at the thought of him because I knew, deep in my heart, I loved him, too, and I had hurt him.

Can a woman love two men?

While the *kimchi* stew bubbled on the stove, I set to getting the rice ready to cook. I'd just started rinsing it when my phone chimed. Picking it up, I saw a text from Jintae saying he'd be home in half an hour. Perfect. Everything would be ready by then.

Right as the rice beeped it was done, I heard the code being entered on the door's security pad. I stopped, not sure what to do. Should I run to him and throw my arms around him, or should I pretend I didn't hear it and scoop the rice from the rice maker?

The door opened, and Jintae called out my name.

"I'm in the kitchen!" I shouted. His footsteps echoed as he came around the corner and headed towards me. My heart thudded in my chest.

When he came into view, I couldn't move. He was here. God, I'd missed him.

I forced myself to take a single step, and he met me there, wrapping his arms around me. The scent of strawberry candy surrounded me. He squeezed me against him and pressed his lips to mine. I melted in his embrace. He drew back. "God, I missed you so much."

"I missed you, too," I said. "I—I made dinner. I hope you like it."

"It smells wonderful. *Kimchi* stew?"

I nodded. And then he was kissing me again, backing me up against the counter by the very spot Young Sik had . . . well, I didn't want to think about that now.

"I could take you right here," he murmured, his hardness pressing against me.

The heat rose to my face. "H-here?" I gulped. He rolled his eyes, and I continued, "Jintae, I need to talk to you."

He put a finger to my lips. "Later. First we eat, then we fuck. You can tell me you love him later."

My jaw dropped open. But, of course, he knew. Why wouldn't he?

"I'm starving," he said with a smirk. "Let's eat." He released me and grabbed four bowls from the cabinet above my head. "You scoop the rice. I'll handle the stew."

I swallowed and nodded, taking the smaller bowls from him.

"What?" he asked. "You thought I didn't know? Come on, Lindsey, you gushed every time you mentioned him. I'm not naïve, you know. I know you have feelings for him."

"Jintae, I—" What could I say?

He patted the top of my head. "It's okay. I'm not mad. You don't need to apologize or anything. But I'm gonna have to sterilize this counter before I use it."

I let out a guffaw. "I have cleaned it several times. That was weeks ago."

"Good to know, but I'm still gonna do it." He flicked my nose with a grin. "You're so cute when you're feeling guilty. Come on. Let's eat."

We sat in silence to eat. I guess it tasted good, because Jintae inhaled two bowls of the stew.

"*Omo,*" he exclaimed, setting his empty bowl on the table. "I am stuffed. That was delicious."

After we cleaned up the dishes, Jintae popped a strawberry candy in his mouth and offered one to me. "These are mints," he said as I took one. "Come on. This way."

He led me toward his bedroom, rolling the strawberry mint around in his mouth. I assumed the bedroom was our destination, but, instead, he stopped right in front of the door and swung me before him, so I stood facing him with the shelf-lined hallway wall at my back. Behind me, five feet of the wall was bare before the shelving started.

"Take off your clothes," he said and pulled his shirt over his head.

"Here?" I asked, confused. "Before we go in?"

He shook his head. "We're not going in my room." And he undid his pants. I followed his actions, still confused, but every time I opened my mouth to question him. He shushed me with a finger to my lips. "No talking."

When we were both nude, he crunched his candy, then he turned me around and shoved me against the wall, pressing my cheek to the paint. It was cool against my skin. He didn't shove me hard, but he held me in place with his palm against my cheek and his body against mine.

"Jintae, what—?"

"Shh. Didn't I say no talking? The only thing I want to hear coming out of your mouth is moaning when I fuck you."

Lightning raced from my heart to my belly at his words.

His minty breath washed over me as he kissed my earlobe and raked his teeth along the edge. Just like he wanted, I moaned.

Still pressing my cheek against the wall with his hand, he traced kisses along my jaw and down the nape of my neck and my spine. I closed my eyes, concentrating on every little sensation his lips and teeth made.

His free hand drifted to my waist. He kicked my legs apart and wrapped his arm around my waist to jerk my ass away from the wall. I braced myself to stop from falling, standing there with my ass sticking out toward him.

"Mm. Nice," he said, rubbing my butt cheeks. "So round. You're beautiful, you know that?"

He took his hand off my face, finally, and pulled my ass even farther from the wall. His dick ran through my slickness before he thrust inside me.

"Oh god. That's so good," he murmured.

A moan escaped me as he slid deeper.

"Yeah. That's what I wanna hear," he said. He slid his hand around the swell of my hip to the folds between my thighs. When he found my clit, he pressed his finger to it, eliciting another groan from me.

He molded himself to me, pulling my hips closer, and plunged even deeper. I pressed my ass against him. We were so close he couldn't pull out without losing contact, so he just kept thrusting in and in and in, all the while teasing my clit with his finger.

It didn't take long for an orgasm to rock my body. I clenched around him as tightly as I had done to Young Sik, and Jintae grunted, forcing himself through my tight folds.

"Holy shit," he cursed through a clenched jaw, quickening his pace. His hand left my clit, and he wrapped his arm around my stomach, pulling us closer than I thought possible. When he exploded inside me, I felt every little spasm.

"Holy fuck, Lindsey," he said, still clutching me, his breathing harsh in my ear. "That was amazing."

I smiled as I sank to the floor, the energy leaving me in a rush. He was right. It was amazing.

Chapter Twenty-Three

Friday, I had an appointment I had to keep: photography for a big drama. To celebrate after the shooting, Anne and I went out for drinks and girl time. Jintae told me not to worry, he would spend time with his friends, whom he hadn't seen since leaving for the tour.

Anne and I tried a new pub that had opened in Young Sik's neighborhood. The *soju* was cheap and the food excellent. Before I knew it, we were both piss drunk and laughing so hard at ourselves we could barely talk.

The place was busy, and we had trouble keeping the wolves at bay. A man walked toward us with a drunken swagger and tried to solicit us for a *ménage à trois*. When we politely declined, he not-so-politely tried to lay his hand on Anne and ended up with a knee to the junk for his trouble. The bar's owner escorted him from the building.

As he was being walked out, Young Sik walked in, giving the men a curious glance. Then his gaze fell on me and his face lit up.

"Fancy meeting you here," he exclaimed. "May I?"

I patted the seat beside me. "Please. We could use a real man right about now."

Anne snickered and threw back another shot of *soju*. "Especially one as gorgeous as you," she told him.

Young Sik gave her a lopsided grin. I called for another glass and bottle.

"You two are absolutely schnockered," he noted.

"Nah." I waved my hand around, watching it a second as it blurred in front of me. "Uh . . . we're perfectly fine."

His glass came, and I filled it with the new bottle. "See? Steady as a rock." I nearly spilled the last little bit. "Oops."

He shared a couple of drinks with us until it was obvious even to me I was drunker than I ever remembered being.

He stood. "I think it's time to go. I'll pay the tab." Despite my protests, he plodded over to the register to pay.

Outside, we watched Anne get into a taxi, clearly able to hold her liquor better than me. Young Sik raised a hand to hail a taxi for me, but I stopped him.

"Let's walk instead," I insisted. "I need some fresh air and it's a nice night." Plus, I wanted to stay with him a little longer. I missed him.

"Are you sure you can?" he asked.

I nodded, but that wasn't the best thing to do as the world tilted. I leaned into him for support. "I'm fine, really." My gorge threatened to rise, but I pushed the feeling back down.

Once we got going, I walked okay.

"So, how have you been?" I asked.

He shrugged. "All right, I guess. You?"

138

"Mm. Same."

"You and Jintae all right?" There was an edge to his voice, like he was asking something he really didn't want a positive answer to.

"Oh. Yeah. We're fine. Peachy, even." I forced a smile, feeling guilty that I was happy with Jintae.

"That's good." He stared at his feet as we trudged along.

"I miss you," I started to say, but then I took a step that twisted my ankle and I fell. Young Sik caught me and I sank to the sidewalk. The world wavered.

"Shall I carry you?"

"Huh?" His words caught me off guard.

Young Sik turned, offering his back to me. "Hop on. I'll carry you."

"Oh, don't be silly. This isn't some drama."

"Just get on."

I looked at him squatting with his back to me to offer me a ride.

I felt silly. I really did, but I also didn't think I could take another step, or even stand, so I clambered onto his back. I put my arms around his neck and hung my head over his right shoulder as he stood, hooking his arms beneath my thighs to support my weight.

We traveled like that for a while, not saying anything. His labored breathing worried me. Was I too heavy for him? But when I brought it up, he insisted he was fine.

"I missed you, too," he finally said.

And then the world tilted again. A wave of nausea rolled over me. There was a little city park up ahead with a bench sitting under a mature tree, and I asked him if we could sit for a bit.

"You okay?" he asked.

"No," I squeaked, trying not to throw up on him.

He veered off the sidewalk and onto the grass. We reached the bench, and I clambered off him and threw myself behind the tree to toss my cookies . . . or my alcohol . . . or whatever.

As I kneeled there, hunched over and puking my guts out, I felt a gentle tug on my hair as he pulled it back out of the way.

I was so embarrassed to be doing this in front of him, but also grateful for his help. When I finished, he guided me to the bench, and I sank down on it, the world still spinning.

He looked up and off in the distance, back toward the sidewalk. "There's a convenience store over there. I'll go get you a water. Will you be okay?"

I nodded, putting my head in my hands.

He didn't take long and soon came back with a bottle of water, a handful of napkins, and a roll of mints. God, he thought of everything!

I swished some water around in my mouth and spit it out, before taking a few deep swallows from the bottle. Young Sik handed me the mints and took back the water, using it to dampen a napkin. As I sucked on a couple mints, he dabbed at my face. The coolness of the wet napkin was refreshing.

He had leaned in close to me to wipe something from the corner of my mouth when I heard someone cry out, *"YA!"*

A very familiar someone.

We both jerked our heads in the direction of the shout to see Jintae storming our way, his face dark with anger. As he neared us, Young Sik rose to greet him, only to receive a fist to the mouth that sent him to his knees with blood splattering me.

"Jintae!" I cried out as he dove after Young Sik, murder in his eyes. "No!" I staggered to my feet and reached for him. At the same time, he pulled his arm back to punch Young Sik, and his elbow connected with my face.

With a cry, I fell backwards, hitting my head on the bench. Pain flared through me.

When I could focus, I saw Jintae and Young Sik frozen with looks of horror on their faces. Jintae still had his elbow pulled back, his other hand fisting Young Sik's t-shirt, holding him for a second punch. But his eyes, wide as saucers, were focused on me, as were Young Sik's. Then time started again, and both men clambered over each other to get to me. I sat up, putting a hand to my nose as a hot, thick wetness gushed over my lips. My fingers came away covered in crimson.

"Jintae!" I screamed. "You broke my nose!"

I didn't know if that was actually the case, but it sure hurt enough to be.

"Oh my god, Lindsey, I'm so sorry!" Jintae paled as he squatted beside me. His words spewed forth in a panic. "Oh my god, I didn't mean to hit you. *Aish!* You're bleeding. We need to get you to a hospital."

"What the fuck were you doing?!" I was still in scream mode. "My god, Jintae! Fuck. Help me up."

Young Sik interjected. "That wouldn't be a good idea. You're drunk. Lay back and I'll call one-one-nine."

"No. I'll be fine." I tried to rise to my feet using a paralyzed Jintae for support. The world tilted and went black.

Chapter Twenty-Four

I knew where I was even before I opened my eyes. A hospital. I peeled my eyes open, groaning. My head felt three times its size and stuffed with cotton.

As soon as I raised my lids, the guys were on me. Both were here, which surprised me but also made me happy. Were they getting along now?

Jintae grabbed my left hand. "Lindsey? How are you feeling?"

I groaned again and turned my head his way. Young Sik peeked over Jintae's shoulder at me.

I struggled to sit. "I feel like shit," I said, my voice hoarse. "Can we go home now?"

"The doctor wants to keep you overnight."

"No!" I shouted a little louder than I meant to, causing them to jump. "Sorry. No. I want to go home."

"I'll go fetch the doc," Jintae said and darted out of the room.

After he left, I gave Young Sik a weary smile. "Did you two make up?" I asked, touching my face. God, it felt super swollen under my fingertips and was especially sensitive around my nose.

"He thought I was trying to kiss you. After I told him what I'd actually been doing to you, he backed down."

"I'm surprised you both came with me."

"He was so upset about you he couldn't drive. I drove you guys here."

"That sounds just like Jintae." I couldn't help but snicker. "Anyway, thank you."

Just then, Jintae came back in the room followed by the doctor, who gave me a quick bow and introduced himself.

"How are you feeling?" the doctor asked. "Your guardian says you wish to go home."

"Yes, please. I'm feeling much better, and I'd like to leave."

He stared at my chart, frowning. "Hmm. You have no concussion, and your nose isn't broken, so you should be okay to leave. But I'd advise you to stay a little longer and get some rest because of your, ahem, drinking earlier."

"I'd just like to go, please," I said.

He sighed and turned to Jintae. "She can go but monitor her for a few more hours to make sure she's okay." He turned back to me. "If any of your pain worsens or if you get a headache, return to make sure your condition hasn't worsened."

"I understand," I said. "Thank you."

Jintae went off again to pay for the visit while Young Sik helped me gather my things.

"Are you sure you'll be okay?" he asked.

"If you come with us, I think I'll be all right."

He grinned at me.

When I arrived home, I immediately crashed on the couch. The last thing I remembered was the guys settling to either side of me, and Jintae turning on the television.

I awoke sometime later to find that my head was resting in Jintae's lap and my legs were curled around Young Sik.

Jintae sat with his head resting on a fist, his elbow propped up on the arm rest. His eyes were closed, his breathing relaxed. As I lifted my head, I saw Young Sik lay diagonally across the couch, his upper body draped across the back with his mouth open. He snorted and opened his eyes when I attempted to sit.

My head still felt stuffy and heavy, but not as bad as it had been. Jintae helped me up and rubbed his eyes.

"What time is it?" he asked.

Young Sik reached for his phone on the coffee table while I glanced outside. Low morning sunlight streamed through the windows.

"About seven," Young Sik answered and yawned.

I felt gross. "I need a shower," I said and rose unsteadily to my feet.

"I'll help you," Jintae said.

Young Sik replied, "I'll go get breakfast."

My stomach growled, and I got a sudden craving. "I want waffles."

He pointed a finger at me. "No. You're getting *haejang-guk*."

I didn't want hangover soup. "Waffles. Apple."

"No."

"Oh, come on, Young Sik."

"Actually," Jintae said, "waffles sound fantastic. I'll take strawberry."

Young Sik gave him an incredulous look, then threw up his hands. "Fine. But I'm still buying you *haejang-guk*."

"I'm hungry enough to eat both," I replied before Jintae and I disappeared into his bedroom.

I heard the front door open and close as I stepped onto the tile of Jintae's bathroom.

My first glance in the mirror elicited a shriek from me. "Jintae! Why didn't you tell me my face was so swollen? My god, I don't even look like myself."

I patted at my face, careful not to hurt myself. My upper lip and the area around my nose were puffy. Both of my eyes were black. I swear, I looked like I'd been murdered.

There were still cotton plugs in my nose, which I pulled out, wincing as I cracked the dried blood on each nostril. Tears brimmed in my eyes. One escaped, trickling down my cheek.

Seeing my distress, Jintae pulled me away from the mirror and held me against him. "I'm sorry," he whispered. "This was my fault. I overreacted, and I'm sorry."

We stood like that with the seconds ticking away until I brought my hands up and pushed him away.

"Shower," I mumbled.

He nodded and started the water while I undressed. After turning on the showerhead, he helped me pull my shirt over my head.

146

He started to remove his own clothes, and I stopped him. "What are you doing?"

"I'm going to help you shower. You don't need to be passing out in my bathroom. Besides, I need to wash up, too."

I don't know why, but it seemed awkward stepping into the shower stall with him. I mean, we'd seen each other naked a few times, but, to me, this was different. Plus, I felt like I had a balloon for a head, making me want to run and hide under the covers of my bed . . . or his bed. Either one.

He caught my distress and shifted me around to face him. The water struck his chest and trickled toward his flaccid member. Geez. I was so ugly my naked body wasn't even turning him on.

My breath hitched. Tears stung my eyes. What a stupid thing to cry over. A couple tears escaped and mingled with the shower water on my cheeks.

Jintae hooked a finger under my chin and lifted it until I stared into his eyes. "You're still beautiful," he whispered, seeming to read my thoughts. He placed a delicate kiss on my lips. Then, using his thumb, he wiped the tears away. "Let's get you cleaned up, neh?"

❥ ❧

We were sitting on his bed, him toweling my hair dry, when Young Sik returned.

"Breakfast is here!" he called out. We met him as he reached the end of the hallway. He grinned when he saw us. Looking at me, he said, "I got you *haejang-guk*, but only a half serving so you can enjoy your waffles, too. Oh, and I got you this." He shuffled the bags around and handed me a small, white plastic bag. When I took it, he said, "It's a mask to help with your swelling. Just put it in the fridge while we're eating, and by the time we're done, it should be cold enough."

"Oh! Thank you," I said, touched by the kind gesture. Young Sik had to be the most considerate man I knew. I took the mask out. It was round with holes for your eyes, nose and mouth and filled with a gel. As the guys set everything out to eat, I read the instructions and put the mask in the fridge.

I ate the soup first. *Haejang-guk* was a hearty beef stew filled with napa cabbage, radish, onion, and mushroom. I felt better after finishing it, and I admitted that to Young Sik who replied, "Told you so."

After breakfast, Young Sik left as he had things to do. Jintae suggested I take the mask out of the fridge and try it.

"You can use my bed. I'll lie with you."

I couldn't refuse that invitation. I was getting tired, so we took a nap together.

I awoke to my face pressed against Jintae's chest, the mask askew. I tore it from my head, which didn't feel quite like a balloon anymore. My lips had returned to their normal size.

I rolled onto my back stared at the ceiling only to realize I had to pee. My attempt to sit up and get out of bed roused Jintae. He sat up and looked over at me, blinking, his blonde hair tousled like a fuzzy kitten. "Where are you going?"

"Bathroom," I replied and sort of fell out of bed, much to my chagrin. Jintae barely covered a chuckle.

After I did my business, I checked out my face in the mirror. While my eyes still looked like I hadn't slept in days, the rest of my face had almost returned to normal. There was still swelling around my nose, and my cheeks were puffy, but overall I thought I could go out in public with a generous application of Jintae's makeup.

When I returned to the bedroom, Jintae was still in bed leaning back against the headboard and playing on his phone. He wore no shirt. I was sure he'd been wearing one before. The blankets covered him to his waist.

He looked up and grinned at me, placing his phone back on the bedside table.

"Come sit next to me," he said and patted the bed.

"Aren't we getting up?"

"Not yet. Come here."

"Why?"

He threw the covers back to reveal his nude body. "Because I wanna . . ." He let the words drift off. "That is, if you want to."

I ran my eyes ran along him, taking everything in. He wasn't muscular, but he was fit. His body smooth and slender with just a hint of abs. The scar above his heart just added to his appeal. And he was erect . . . for me. It made me feel wanted again. I couldn't help but stare at his hard member, admiring the girth and length of it.

I swallowed, and the moisture pooled between my thighs just at the sight of him. I shed my clothes and crawled onto the bed, feeling clumsy. He guided me beside him and I lay on my back. He moved to lean over me, his arms supporting his weight on either side of my head.

"You're looking much better," he said, studying my face with an intensity that made me blush and avert my eyes. "Shy now?"

I shrugged. And then his lips were on mine. When I opened my mouth to accept him, I could still taste the strawberry on his tongue. It made me wonder if he always tasted like this. Just like Young Sik always tasted like chocolate.

Oh god, why was I thinking of Young Sik right now? I pushed the thought away.

"I'm going to take my time with you," Jintae murmured after pulling away. He trailed kisses along my cheek and my neck, stopping at my breasts to give attention to each one.

I entwined my fingers in his hair and kissed the top of his head, moaning as tendrils of heat curled through my belly.

His hand drifted along my skin and rested on my thigh as he worked. With my nerves on fire, I felt every brief touch, my body swaying and bucking beneath him.

His fingers delved between my folds. "You're so wet," he breathed. "I need a taste."

Kisses trailed down my belly and along my thigh. He positioned himself between my splayed legs and slid his hands beneath my ass cheeks to lift me toward him for the buffet.

Teasing, he kissed the delicate, shaven flesh around my most sensitive parts, eliciting a moan from me. I'd let go of him as he'd moved south, but now my fingers twisted in his hair once again as I lifted my hips to press my snatch against his mouth.

His tongue darting between my folds sent jolts of electricity through me. My grip on him tightened. God, he felt so good.

His tongue swept toward my clit and he swirled it around the sensitive nub before sealing his lips over it. I gasped and bucked beneath him as the orgasm inched itself closer.

As he worked, he used two fingers to part my folds. He slipped them inside me, something for me to clench when the waves of the orgasm broke under the work of his tongue. I jolted, pushing his face into me as I rode the orgasmic waves, gasping and screaming his name as my pussy contracted around his fingers, trying to pull them deeper and milking them as if they were a dick ready to come.

After I settled and released his hair, he lifted his head, grinning at me. "Did you like that?" He pulled his fingers out of me.

I nodded, my mouth spread in a wide smile. "Oh god, yes."

He crawled up my body until he hovered over me again. The scent of sex and strawberries permeated the air around me.

Without warning, he rammed himself deep inside me, eliciting a squeal from me that made him give me a savage look.

"I thought you were going to take it slow?" I said, breathless.

He shrugged. "Maybe you're too much for me to take slow. I need all of me inside you." He thrust himself further. "God, you're heaven to me."

I wrapped my legs around him, opening myself to give him full access. He took advantage of that, sliding in and out through the folds within me.

His lips met mine as he moved, attacking my mouth with his own until a contraction of my muscles made him bury his face in my hair with a groan.

It didn't take long for him to spasm inside me. When he pulled out, he collapsed beside me, drawing me into his fiery embrace. "God, Lindsey, I love you so much it hurts." His arms tightened around me. "Stay with me," he whispered. "Don't ever leave me."

Chapter Twenty-Five

We returned to work Monday. Luckily for me, makeup covered what hadn't healed on my injured face, and I could avoid answering embarrassing questions.

I had a backlog of clients because of my time off and worked late into the night over the next two weeks to catch up, only taking off Sunday.

Jintae was just as busy, planning various fan signs and doing commercials and posing for ads and magazine shoots. As a result, we barely saw each other over the two weeks following our vacation.

On the second Sunday after returning to work, we planned a quiet day to enjoy each other's company at home. That included ordering pizza delivery for dinner.

When the pizza arrived, Jintae went to the door to fetch it while I grabbed plates, glasses, and *soju*. Jintae promised me he wouldn't elbow my face this time if I drank too much, then skirted off toward the door before I hit him.

We had just set everything up on the table to enjoy our meal when someone knocked on the door. Thinking it was a neighbor or the pizza man returning because he forgot something, I told Jintae to sit and dish out the pizza while I answered the door.

I looked through the peephole, only to see Young Sik standing in the hallway. I opened the door. "What brings you here?"

He stood there with an embarrassed look on his face. I noticed he had a couple of suitcases sitting on either side of him.

"What are the bags for?" I asked.

"Can I speak to Jintae for a minute?"

Just then, the man in question popped his head over my shoulder, greeting him in English. "Hey man, wassup?"

I stepped aside to let them speak.

Young Sik gave a polite bow to Jintae and asked, "Might I stay here for a couple weeks? My apartment building is being renovated and I have no place to stay."

"So suddenly?" I asked.

He turned my way. "There was an electrical fire in one of the apartments above mine Friday night. They need to do extensive repairs, so everyone has to go."

"Oh my! Are you okay?" I asked, my hands flying to my mouth.

"Yes. I'm fine. There was no damage to my apartment, but they are redoing most of the wiring in my part of the building."

"What about your stuff? Your furniture and all that?"

"They're storing it for everyone. I just need a place to crash until repairs are done. They're estimating two weeks right now. So . . . may I?"

Jintae's face broke out into a huge grin. "Of course you may! Come on in. Lindsey's sleeping with me now, so you can have her old room."

Young Sik looked relieved. "I don't want to be any trouble. I can stay on the couch."

"Nonsense! A man needs his privacy. Come on. Let's get you settled."

I'll be honest. Jintae's kindness surprised me. Not that I didn't expect him to have a charitable soul—after all, he took me in—but that he was willing to let Young Sik share his home despite knowing we'd had a relationship and that I still had feelings for him.

As we walked past the dining room table, Young Sik gasped. "Did I interrupt your dinner? I'm sorry."

Jintae waved his concern away. "No big deal. Lindsey, grab an extra plate and glass for him while I show him to his room."

❦

We fell into a comfortable routine. Our schedules were similar enough that we could enjoy a late dinner together most nights. Jintae and Young Sik bonded during our late-night meal, becoming good friends, even talking about releasing a song together.

After a week, Young Sik's apartment management realized the damage was more extensive than they thought and expanded the renovation time to a month. I can't say any of us were disappointed to hear that.

With Jintae's workaholic personality, after the first week, he resumed his routine of staying in his studio until deep into the night, giving Young Sik and I many days together alone. You might think that since we still loved each other, I might cheat on Jintae with him, but you would be wrong. Instead, we spent our evenings playing video games or watching television when we weren't busy doing our own things. Oh, sure, I'd often lay my head in Young Sik's lap as we lounged on the couch, and he sometimes played with my hair, but that's as far as it went between us. We were content to be near each other.

Then, after the second week, I got two packages of men's underwear in the mail with an invitation to apply to be a guest photographer for one of the biggest male underclothes makers in Korea, Kilo Fashions.

And that changed everything.

Chapter Twenty-Six

I sat on the couch one evening with YouTube streaming music videos while I opened the shipping box that sat on the coffee table. Young Sik walked in from his bedroom and plopped on the cushion next to me.

"Oh! What's in the box?"

I grinned and pulled out two packages of men's bikini underwear.

He cocked his head, giving me a questioning look. "Panties?"

(Before you laugh, understand that "panties" is Korean for either women's or men's underwear.)

I nodded and my grin got wider. "They have chosen me to apply for a chance at being a guest photographer for Kilo Fashions. If I win, ads featuring my photos will appear in some of Korea's most acclaimed fashion magazines."

His face lit up. "Really? That's amazing!"

"Wanna model a pair for me?"

He plucked the black pair from my hand and shrugged. "Sure."

Jintae popped up next to him. I hadn't even heard him come in from work. He snatched the package from Young Sik. "What are these? Panties? Where's mine?"

"I have two pair," I said, holding the other package out to him. "Wanna model for me, too?"

"Oh, hell yeah!" He threw the black package back at Young Sik and grabbed the one I held out to him. "Wait. Model for what?"

I told him what I'd told Young Sik. Then I looked from one guy to the other. "How about a provocative team up? Something a little risqué?"

They exchanged glances. Jintae's face broke out into a grin and Young Sik mirrored him.

"We can do that," Young Sik told me. "After all, we were both idols. We're used to lying all over each other." I thought I saw an extra gleam in his eye at the thought of Jintae lying on him.

We decided to do a photoshoot Friday night.

Chapter Twenty-Seven

I set everything up on Friday while the guys got themselves ready. I hung a white backdrop behind Jintae's cream colored couch and set up a tripod with one camera while keeping another on a strap around my neck for mobile shots.

When the guys strode into the room, I was thankful my camera was on a strap, for it slipped from my fingers when I laid my eyes on them.

Jintae had teased his longish blonde locks. His face was flawless with black eyeliner, a touch of blush, and pink lip gloss. He had chosen the white bikini briefs which rendered his exposed skin almost as pale as my own in the bright studio lights. He had taken no effort to hide his scar, which glowed pink in the light. I thought it added to his sexiness, and I had to stop myself from running my fingers over it as he approached. Overall, he resembled a playboy who had just got done playing.

Contrasting him, Young Sik's darker skin tone complimented the black briefs. His makeup was plainer than Jintae's, but no less stunning. He had his dark hair slicked back and freshly shaved on the sides. A single lick curled over his eyes. With his mouth pulled into a frown, he looked like he might murder me without a thought.

Lightning zipped along my skin at the thought, leaving goosebumps in its wake.

And Young Sik was ripped. I mean, Jintae had abs, but he was soft compared to Young Sik, who appeared to be all muscle and sinew.

"Might want to close your mouth," Jintae said, "before you drool all over my white carpet."

I snapped my jaw shut, heat flushing from my neck to my cheeks. *Way to be professional, Lindsey.*

When the guys transformed into model mode, they were different people. Their faces became slack and a bit haughty. As I snapped shot after shot, they ran through several poses. We started with them standing in front of the couch and ended with them sitting on it. Having two of K-pop's sexiest guys draped over the couch and each other in view of my lens was an experience I'd never forget. But what came after . . . I doubt anyone else in the world would ever experience it.

"You should join us," Young Sik said. I think he said it as a joke while I packed my handheld camera away, but Jintae started nodding his head.

"Yes. You can wear that cute little number I bought you the other day."

"You bought her a cute little number?" Young Sik raised his eyebrows.

I shook my head at Jintae, ignoring Young Sik. "No way. I'm a photographer, not a model. I prefer to stay behind the lens."

"Oh, come on!" Jintae gave me a pleading look. "Just for fun. It's not like we haven't seen you naked before. Besides, you have an amazing body!" He looked me up and down to prove it.

My cheeks got hot. I looked from one guy to the other, then threw up my hands as they grinned at me. "Fine!"

Jintae helped me get ready while Young Sik made a trip to the half bath to freshen up.

I wasn't much for makeup. That was Anne's area of expertise, so Jintae helped me put on enough to bring out the color of my eyes and to show off the freckles that dusted my cheeks and nose.

The lingerie set he had bought me barely covered my assets. It consisted of an emerald satin thong and a matching camisole that didn't quite cover my tits.

"Are you sure you want Young Sik to see me in this?" I asked, peering at myself in the mirror. I had to admit I looked pretty hot. The emerald complimented my red hair, and it made my green eyes pop.

Jintae came up behind me, putting his arms around me. I had my hair done up in a messy bun and he brushed a stray stand away to kiss my ear. "Why not?" he asked. Our eyes met in the mirror. His lips tipped up into a smile that sent electricity straight to my core. Then he winked at me. *Dead. I am totally dead now.* My heart fluttered in my chest.

When we sauntered back into the living room, Young Sik lounged on the couch. He leaned forward and raised an eyebrow. "Wow," was all he said.

I set the tripod camera up to take a photo every three seconds, making sure it focused on the entire couch. The guys sat with enough space between them for me to slide into, and then we began.

I wasn't sure what to do, so Jintae took my arm and draped it over his shoulders. "Look at me like you want to fuck me," he said.

I laughed, but he remained serious. So, putting on my best "fuck me" face, I lay back against him and stared over my shoulder into his eyes. The camera snapped shots.

He pulled me into his lap and more shots were taken. I draped myself across both men, shuddering as their hands touched my naked skin. We went through several provocative poses.

Somehow, I ended up on Young Sik's lap, facing forward with his tongue wrapped around my ear and his hand slipping under the too-short camisole to cup my left breast. I let out a moan of pleasure before I realized what I had done. My eyes moved to glance at Jintae, expecting him to be ready to explode. Instead, he stared at us in wonder, his tongue slowly running across his lower lip.

"That's hot," he whispered as the camera continued to click away. He looked Young Sik in the eye. "I want you to do her."

My jaw dropped. Moisture collected between my thighs. "Jintae, are you serious?" I asked. Was he setting me up for something?

"Totally serious," he replied. "I want him to fuck you as you sit on him."

A flash of lightning surged through me. "I never knew you were a voyeur."

"I'm not. Who says I'm just going to watch?"

Oh god.

When I stood so Young Sik could slip out of his briefs, my legs could barely hold me up. Were we really going to do this?

I noticed Jintae's eyes widen, and I glanced behind me. Young Sik stood naked in all his glory.

"You can take all of that?" Jintae asked, his eyes unabashedly on Young Sik's long-ass dick.

I averted my eyes and gave a small incline of my head.

"Well, damn, girl, let's get this party started!"

I started to pull the camisole over my head, but Jintae stopped me. "Keep it on. It's hot. And we can just move the thong out of the way."

Oh god. I gushed again.

Young Sik situated himself on the couch and motioned for me to sit on his lap. He remained silent throughout the entire exchange.

"Are you sure you want me to do this?" I asked Jintae.

"Now more than ever," he said. He waved his hand at me. "Go on now."

As I lowered myself onto Young Sik's lap, he grabbed my hip with one hand while using the other to guide himself inside me, taking a moment to pull the string of my thong aside. I was so wet, he slipped right in. I groaned at the sensation of his long dick parting my folds.

He attacked my ear with his tongue before sucking on it. His breathing was loud and sexy in my ear as he worked.

And then Jintae leaned over me—us—and brushed his lips over mine. I opened myself to him and he delved inside, his tongue dancing with mine.

Young Sik cupped my breast beneath the camisole again and pushed against me, lifting me up as he thrust inside me. He grunted, and I imagined him with his eyes closed, sweat beading on his forehead. Fuck. I was getting close to coming already.

Jintae pulled away and trailed kisses down my neck and collarbone. He pushed the silky fabric of the camisole up and took the nipple of my other breast—the one not occupied by Young Sik's hand—into his mouth.

The sensation was too much. I moaned and my fingers laced in Jintae's hair as he continued his journey south, feathering kisses along my belly and down to my thighs. He slid off the couch and positioned himself between two pairs of legs, Young Sik's and mine.

I felt the fabric of my thong get shoved aside. My breath hitched. When I peered down at him, Jintae was gazing up at me. His tongue darted out between his teeth and he held it there, his lips tipping into a malicious grin.

Using his fingers, he parted my folds and touched the tip of his tongue to my clit. I bucked upwards. My fingers gripped the back of his head and pulled him into me. All the while, I felt the steady thrust of Young Sik. I clenched my muscles around him and he moaned in my ear.

My heart throbbed in my chest, pulsating with every touch and thrust. The nerves of my skin crackled with electricity, begging to be caressed.

As if sensing this, Young Sik ran his hand up from my hip to cup my other breast while sliding the other hand up to grasp my chin. He pulled my head back against him with his thumb rubbing across my lower lip. Shockwaves jolted through me, sending ripples of goosebumps along my flesh.

Meanwhile, Jintae's tongue went to work on my most sensitive nub. His fingers no longer held my folds open. As I neared an orgasm, I felt a fluttering lower between my legs. Young Sik tensed and groaned, and I realized Jintae had begun to pleasure him as well, cupping his balls.

Jintae's tongue pushed me toward the cliff of my orgasm. I tried to resist, tried to hold it off for a few seconds more, but one final lick followed by Young Sik's hard thrust shoved me over the edge and I fell, my body bucking between the two men, my muscles clenching hard on Young Sik's dick. My screams of pleasure filled the air as I reached to grab anything—Jintae's hair, Young Sik's hands, any piece of flesh I could get my hands on.

"Oh fuck." Young Sik stiffened beneath me and thrust himself as deep as he could. "Oh god."

I felt him spasm as he came inside me.

Meanwhile, Jintae laid his cheek on my thigh, his eyes closing and euphoria spreading across his face, basking in the moment with us. His breathing was just as ragged as ours.

Young Sik's voice echoed in my ear. "That was amazing."

Jintae nodded. "It was." He sat up and looked at the floor between us. "Aw fuck. I jizzed all over my couch."

Chapter Twenty-Eight

I walked out of the bathroom, toweling my hair dry. Jintae and Young Sik sat on Jintae's bed, my laptop open on Jintae's lap.

"You guys find the perfect photos for me to send?" I asked, snickering as I knew they were likely engrossed in the *other* photos instead.

Jintae looked my way. "I think we did," he said with that mischievous grin. "We moved our choices to the top of the folder."

I squeezed onto his lap, settling the laptop on my knees. Young Sik leaned forward, a lopsided grin on his face. "Go on and look," he said.

The first four photos weren't that bad as far as choices went. The guys had a pretty good eye, and I might even use one or two of them for my submission. But when I revealed the fifth photo, I let out a guffaw and shook my head, sputtering, "N-no. No no no!"

"Oh, come on," Jintae said in my ear, making me shudder. "It's the best one." They both laughed.

I held up a finger. "Okay, not only am I *not* a model but also this photo is totally inappropriate."

"I want a copy to put on my phone," Young Sik said.

I gasped. "Absolutely not!"

My god. The photo they had chosen showed me sitting on Young Sik's lap, his cock buried deep inside me while he held me back against his chest, one hand on my jaw and the other on a breast. Jintae kneeled in front of us, exposing his nice ass to the camera (and, damn, it was hot!) while he ate me out. It made me flush just looking at it.

"I want to do this again," Young Sik said with no shame. And Jintae agreed with him!

I hid my face in my hands, trying not to drop the computer off my lap as I turned to press myself against Jintae's bare chest. "Oh, god. I can't believe we did that."

Jintae's words breathed in my ear. "I want to be buried deep inside you while Young Sik gets us both off."

More heat rushed to my face. "Good god, guys. Don't. Not now."

"Are you embarrassed?" Jintae asked, gripping my chin and forcing my head up to look at him. I nodded the best I could in his grasp. He grinned and kissed the tip of my nose. "So cute."

I rolled my eyes and tore my face from his grasp. In the process, the laptop tipped and slid off my lap.

"Oh no!" I made a clumsy grab for it, but only made things worse as my knees jerked.

Young Sik reached out and snatched the computer out of the air as it fell. He closed the cover and set it between us on the bed.

"That was close. Thank you," I said. I grabbed it and clutched it to me. "I need to go work on the photos for the shoot." And with that, I slipped out of the room and headed toward the dining room table. The guys didn't follow me. Thank god.

The next morning, I awoke with Jintae wrapped around me. After choosing and editing the photos I planned to send to Kilo, I'd returned to the bedroom to find Jintae and Young Sik poring over Jintae's extensive record collection. Seeing me enter, Young Sik had retired to his bedroom, and Jintae and I crawled into bed. He made love to me slowly that night, and when I woke up in the morning, I was still content from the night before. Then the memory of what I'd done with both guys returned to me and the room got hotter.

Behind me, Jintae stirred and tightened his embrace, snuggling against me. "You're awake?" he whispered in my ear. When I didn't answer, he lifted his head. "You okay?"

"Yeah. Just thinking."

"About what?"

"Last night." I was so embarrassed that my words came out in a forced whisper.

"Did you like it?"

"Would you be angry if I did?" That was my biggest fear. I mean, I had sex with Young Sik right in front of Jintae.

Jintae forced me to face him. His eyes searched my face. "Why would I be angry?"

"Come on. I . . . we . . . Young Sik and I . . ." I couldn't complete the sentence.

"Lindsey, I asked you to do it. Of course I'm not angry. The whole thing was hot, and I want to do it again. I mean, if you're willing, of course."

My cheeks heated. They probably matched my hair color by now. I whispered my answer so low he didn't catch it, and I had to repeat myself. "I liked it. I liked it a lot, and I want to do it again." Just the thought of having Young Sik's face between my legs while Jintae pounded me from behind excited me.

His hand wandered and slipped into my panties. "You're so wet right now," he breathed. "Does it turn you on that much?"

I nodded, words failing me again. When I met his gaze, the room got several degrees warmer.

He pushed me on my back and disappeared beneath the sheets.

His tongue went to work on me, coaxing me to an orgasm quicker than expected. As I bucked against him, he held me to his face until I calmed and relaxed back into the sheets. Then he flipped me over and took me from behind, his girth running through my still-sensitive folds.

A knock sounded on the door. Jintae paused and called out, "What?"

The door opened, and I scrambled to pull away from Jintae to cover myself, but he held me. "You're not going anywhere," he growled.

169

Young Sik stuck his head in the room. "*Ya,* I'm going to order . . . oh, should I come back later?"

To my surprise, Jintae replied, "Join us and we'll go out for breakfast afterward."

I swung my head around. He met my eyes with a twinkle and a wink. "Fuck me," I swore, sinking my head into the pillows to hide my flushed cheeks. At this point, I wondered if they would just stay pink forever with all this constant embarrassment.

We convened in the living room. Jintae wanted to fuck me in the same spot he and I had done it the first time. Just remembering that night made me wet all over again.

"How are we going to do this?" Young Sik asked as we stood naked around that spot.

Jintae took over, leading me to the wall. He faced me toward it. "Brace yourself with your hands." After I placed them on the wall, he pulled my hips toward him until I felt the hardness of his cock poke my ass. "That should be about right. Young Sik, you go around to her front and do whatever you want to her."

I opened my eyes wide and shot Jintae a glance, but he only chuckled and gave my butt cheeks a slap.

Young Sik slipped himself between my arms. Since he was taller than me, he had to duck to reach my lips. His soft kisses soon made me melt into him.

With a push from behind, Jintae entered me, filling me and making me moan into Young Sik's mouth. The rapper's tongue wrestled with mine and his hands trailed down my sides to settle above Jintae's on my hips.

Jintae moved his hands to my shoulders and brought me upright until I molded to his body. He wrapped his arms around my stomach and thrust even deeper into me, his breath echoing in my ears.

Young Sik, meanwhile, feathered my chin and neck with kisses, sinking to his knees and trailing his lips across my breasts, along my stomach, and finally settling between my legs. His tongue darted out, and I gasped, gushing wetness around Jintae's cock. Jintae adjusted his grip on me, sliding his right arm up to encircle my breasts. He twisted my right nipple between his fingers as he ran his tongue along my ear, forcing a moan from my lips.

When Young Sik stopped what he was doing, I glanced down only to see him bring a finger up and swirl it around my clit. Then he slid it downward through my folds with the pads of his fingers facing him. His fingernails scraped lightly against my sensitive flesh. Before I could question him about what he was doing, he slipped his index finger inside me, between my front pussy wall and Jintae's dick. This time, Jintae and I moaned in unison. But Young Sik didn't stop there. He hooked that finger within me as he took his other hand and raised it toward Jintae's balls. The tightness sent my nerves alight. Then his tongue worked on my clit again. Oh god, it felt so good it took only a minute or two for both Jintae and I to shudder as orgasms swept through us.

Jintae pulled out and sat on the floor, tugging me into his lap. "That was amazing," he said, his arms wrapping around me as he spoke.

Young Sik sat across from us and grinned, his dick pointing at me like a beacon.

"Do you want me to suck you off?" I asked, surprising myself. This was something I didn't like to do, but his dick was so hard and so long that I wanted to lick it like a lollipop.

I half-expected Jintae to argue, but he said, "I wanna watch."

I turned my head. "You really are a voyeur, aren't you?" He just shrugged and grinned.

"Are you serious?" Young Sik asked, rising back to his knees. His attention was on Jintae, not me.

"Well, I don't want you to feel left out," the other man said.

I glanced in his direction and caught his nod and the faint smile ghosting his face. Fuck. He was going to get off on me sucking off another guy. What had gotten into him?

Well, hell, why not?

"You're really okay with this?" I don't know which of us Young Sik directed his question to, but we both nodded.

He shrugged and scooted close to me with his dick bouncing right before my eyes. Now, I've said before that I didn't like to do this sort of thing, but I found myself looking forward to it. It was something I hadn't done with either guy yet.

Young Sik sucked in a sharp breath as I wrapped my fingers around the long length of him and guided him into my mouth. He was so long that even half of him didn't even fit. I had little experience as it was, so I wasn't sure how to handle him.

My gaze trailed up his naked chest to meet up with his. He stared at me, his breath caught in his throat, waiting for me to begin. The way his hair fell over his eyes sent a shock of lightning through me. I drew him out slowly through my lips, using my tongue to cradle the underside of him. When his tip reached my lips, I sucked the pre-cum off it and swirled my tongue on the sensitive underside.

He moaned. His eyes closed, and his head went back as I drew him into my mouth again. By my ear, Jintae's breathing quickened. His erection poked between my legs.

Young Sik's fingers tangled in my hair. I bobbed my head to take him in and out. In and out. My fingers, wrapped around his dick, moved in time with my efforts. As his breathing came faster, so did my movements. His grip tightened in my hair and he pulled me into him, forcing me to take more.

My ass rose from Jintae's lap, and the young CEO thrust himself inside me, working me from behind, his dick hard and thick between my pussy lips. I let out a groan that vibrated on Young Sik's length. God, everything these guys did was the best thing I'd ever felt.

Our movements became one steady action, quickening until Young Sik jerked my head into himself. I swallowed more of him than I thought possible. Thick cum coated the back of my throat as he spasmed in my mouth.

When Young Sik pulled out, Jintae's hand wandered to my clit, stimulating it with his delicate touch. Before I knew it, an intense orgasm shuddered through me as he released his seed inside me, his breathing ragged in my ear.

The three of us collapsed on the floor in a tangle of limbs. Jintae held me from behind while Young Sik encircled us both with his arms and legs.

And then my stomach protested with the loudest growl of hunger it could manage.

Chapter Twenty-Nine

*A*fter two weeks, we had settled into a comfortable routine. Young Sik spent more nights sleeping with us than in his own bed. The men also decided it was okay for me to spend time with one while the other wasn't around. As such, I fell even deeper in love with each of them.

One Saturday, I was home alone and took my laptop to the local café to work on my photos. It was a pleasant day, and I sat at a window table farthest from the door to people-watch as I edited my photos and sipped on iced tea. A half-eaten sandwich lay to the left of my laptop as I clicked and swooped and clicked some more, bringing some behind-the-scenes drama photos into their own.

There were two other laptop users in the café. A man sat at the window closest to the door, facing me. Two empty tables separated us. He wore sunglasses and looked like he was busy typing Korea's next best seller.

Kitty-corner to me, near the register, sat a woman who talked into a Bluetooth receiver, waving her hands around with much animation. I imagined her to be a successful blogger or other influencer.

Smiling to myself that I was working alongside like-minded people, I resumed editing. I took another bite of my sandwich before clicking and swooping again.

Sometime later, the woman left and my phone rang. As I answered it, I noticed the man was packing his laptop up as well.

The caller ID read Young Sik. "Where are you?" he asked. "The house is empty."

"I'm at the Corner Café. It was a nice day, so I decided to get out. You're off work, I take it?"

"Yeah. Stay there, I'll be there in ten minutes."

When Young Sik arrived, he nearly collided with the man and his laptop, who'd been delayed by a phone call of his own. Young Sik bowed and apologized, but the man merely shrugged past him and dashed out the door.

"How rude," the rapper commented, walking up to me. I drained the last of my tea as he leaned over my computer to stare at me. "Tea? I think I'll get a coffee. Want anything?"

"No, I'm good. Thanks."

He leaned in closer with a mischievous twinkle in his eye. "Jintae won't be back for a few more hours. Wanna have some fun?"

I blushed. "Let me pack my stuff."

"Great. I'll get the coffee while I wait. Sure you don't want another tea?"

I started to shake my head, then thought better of it. "Sure. Mango, please."

He nodded and shuffled over to the counter.

A few minutes later, we walked back to the condo, keeping a friendly distance between us as we sipped our drinks.

"So, did I hear you and Jintae are actually doing that collab you guys discussed earlier?" I asked.

"Yeah. I'm working on the song. He said he's too busy to contribute right now, but he'll sing whatever I come up with."

"That's awesome. My two besties singing what will be the greatest song to hit Korea." I giggled and played with my straw.

He chuckled and gave me side glances until I asked him what he was doing.

"You're just so cute," he replied with an upturn of his lips.

Before long we arrived home. After drinking so much tea, I made a beeline for the half bath.

Upon exiting, Young Sik accosted me and slammed me gently against the wall by the kitchen. His lips connected with mine, making me melt into a puddle of goo. He attacked my lips like he was ravenous. When he drew back, breathless, he whispered, "Bedroom," and lifted me into the air. I wrapped my legs around his waist and my arms around his neck as he kissed me again.

He carried me to his bedroom, kicking the door open before depositing me on my feet on the floor by the bed. Our clothes went flying. He slammed the door shut before pushing me onto the bed.

"I've been waiting forever to have you to myself," he said, and asked me to scoot all the way onto the bed until I lay against the pillows. Since the guys had started sharing me, he'd only taken advantage of being alone with me twice in the past two weeks while Jintae had me almost every night, whether or not they paired up to attack me.

I remained silent as he crawled up the length of my body, trailing his fingers along my skin. Goose pimples flared in their wake.

He hovered over me. "Which way do I want you?" he mused. He peppered my cheek and throat with kisses. Electricity surged through me. My fingers dove into his hair, and I brought his lips to mine. He tasted of mocha and chocolate. Our tongues danced until he pulled away. "Roll over on your side. Away from me."

I did as he instructed, my flesh humming with desire. I only wanted him to touch me, to send me over the edge. I'd been waiting forever, too, for him. My heartbeat quickened as he ran the palm of his hand down my side and along the swell of my hip. He took in the scent of my hair and molded himself to me. His hardness poked between my thighs.

Then his hand slipped over my hip to the parting between my thighs. His fingers pushed through my folds to find my clit. I gasped and parted my legs for him. He kissed the back of my neck, the sound of his breath sweet in my ear. When his dick dipped into my slick folds, I groaned. He wrapped his arms around me, flexing his muscles and tightening his grip.

"I feel like I can't get close enough to you," he murmured, pulling me even tighter against him, all the while thrusting deeper and deeper inside me.

My now-neglected clit cried out to be touched again. His hand slid back down and he obliged, coaxing a powerful orgasm from me within seconds. Even the roots of my hair tingled with the electricity it generated. The clenching of my muscles made him grunt, and he pulled out, rolling me onto my back. "I want to watch you while I come," he said, nestling himself between my thighs. My sensitive flesh welcomed every inch of him.

His eyes searched my face, crinkling into perfect crescent moons as they studied me. "You're so beautiful, Lindsey, and right now, in this moment, you belong only to me."

I saw, for just a second, a spark of jealousy in his eyes. A little possession. And I welcomed it. He thrust into me harder and faster. I clenched myself around him, my eyes never leaving his. It was only when he was deep into his orgasm that his eyes finally closed, and he buried his face in my hair, his breath tickling the stray locks along my shoulder.

Afterward, he lay beside me, his arms holding me tightly against him. I lay a hand on his hard abs with my cheek resting against his chest.

"Do you think Jintae would kiss me?" His sudden question took me by surprise.

"Wha—?"

He looked at me, all serious. "During one of our orgies. Do you think he'd kiss me?"

"Would you want him to?" I have to admit, my body heated just thinking about it.

"I'm attracted to him, so, yes, I'd want him to, but I'm afraid to try it. If he doesn't want to do it, he might punch me again."

I snickered. "True dat," I said in English. "Hmm, do you want me to ask him?"

"Could you?" He shifted, his eyes lighting up. "I mean, I'd like it if you could."

I felt like I could talk to Jintae about anything, so this seemed like such a simple thing to ask in theory. The reality of it, though, was a bit different.

Chapter Thirty

When Jintae came home that evening, Young Sik was nowhere to be found. I figured he must have gone out for fresh air, since there was no answer when I knocked on his door for dinner. I sent him a quick text and helped Jintae unwrap the noodles he'd brought. As we worked, I steeled myself to ask him Young Sik's question.

"Jintae," I said, my heart hammering in my chest. Was this going to be harder than I thought?

"Hm?" He looked up from the bag, the last bowl of noodles in his hand.

"Can I ask you something?"

He waited. I swallowed, not sure how to proceed tactfully.

"What is it?" he prompted, his eyebrows raised.

My heart jerked, and I blurted out, "Young Sik wants to kiss you." I winced even before I finished speaking. Way to go, smooth talker. Ugh.

"*Mwo?*" Jintae let the noodles drop to the table. If they hadn't been wrapped so tightly, they might have splattered everywhere.

My face was a furnace. "I mean, um, well . . . you see . . . Young Sik is bi and he—"

"Woah. Woah. Let me stop you right there." He held up his hand, palm out to me before rubbing his forehead with it. "Young Sik . . ." He gave a shake of his head, trying to process the words.

". . . is attracted to you," I finished. "He wants to know if he can kiss you the next time we . . . you know."

The outside door beeped and Young Sik entered the condo. "Something smells good," he exclaimed, sauntering around the corner. "Oh! Noodles!"

As he approached the table, he noticed our stricken faces. My face, which had been so hot before, now drained of the blood heating it, leaving my cheeks chilled.

"What's wrong?" he asked. "Did someone die?" He had a goofy grin on his face that slid away as he looked from Jintae to me. "Okay, what?"

Realization dawned on his face.

Beside me, Jintae's hand curled into a fist. He started to bring it up, but I grabbed it. "Don't you dare. It was an innocent question."

Young Sik held his hands harmlessly in front of him, eyeing Jintae as he said to me, "So, I guess you asked him."

I nodded, lowering my eyes.

He turned to Jintae. "The only reason I asked her to ask you was to avoid the awkwardness. I'm sorry. If you don't want to, I won't pursue it."

"I cannot unlearn this," Jintae said through gritted teeth.

"But you touched my balls the first time we—"

"Just stop," Jintae said. He tensed again.

"Sit," I told him. "Let's just eat. I'm sorry I asked you."

I had to pull on his arm, but he sank into his seat and I settled beside him. I slid a bowl of noodles toward Young Sik. He thanked me and dug in.

The sounds of slurping from both men replaced the awkward silence. I fiddled with my chopsticks, no longer hungry. Jintae was halfway through his meal when he noticed I'd barely touched mine.

"Still can't eat noodles with chopsticks?" he asked, his lips upturning into a brief grin. "Shall I get you a fork?"

"It's not that." I sighed and got up from the table. "I'm not hungry right now."

I headed toward the bedroom, but Jintae grabbed my wrist as I went by. "Don't go," he whispered.

Tilting my head, I looked curiously at him. He stood in front of me and pressed his lips to mine.

Young Sik watched us. He let his chopsticks drop and came around the corner of the table to meet us. With Jintae in front of me, he got behind me, trailing kisses along the nape of my neck and causing shivers to race along my spine. I let out a moan. He kissed along the lobe of my ear and down my cheek to touch his lips to the corner of my mouth as Jintae still wrestled with my tongue.

What happened next surprised all of us, I think, but Young Sik had this way about him to get Jintae to do things he normally would balk at.

Jintae withdrew his tongue, kissing my lips again as Young Sik joined him. They both stood side-by-side at this point. Young Sik moved closer to him and tipped his head so his lips brushed both mine and Jintae's. I drew back just a hair and suddenly the guys were kissing each other. I was so close I felt their breaths mingling. I drew back more and watched, enraptured by Jintae's marshmallow lips as they pressed against Young Sik's thinner ones. Then he opened himself to him and Young Sik dove his tongue inside.

I moaned as lightning struck my loins, making me wet. Fuck, that was hot. I swear, Young Sik could make Jintae do anything. They continued to kiss each other, Young Sik's palms cupping Jintae's jaw. Oh fuck. My knees went weak with desire. Young Sik glanced my way and grabbed my head, pulling me close again. I kissed them as they kissed each other, then I got an idea and dropped to my knees in between them, facing Jintae. His pants slipped to the floor under my nimble fingers, followed by his underwear. When his member sprang free, I took it in my mouth. A sharp gasp escaped him, and he put his hands around my head, pulling me closer so he could go deeper.

It didn't take long for his hot cream to fill my mouth. I think this experience turned him on more than he knew.

When he finished, he gasped, "Bedroom," and we filed in there and onto his bed, shedding clothes along the way.

Jintae positioned me on the bed with my ass in the air and my head in a spot where I could reach Young Sik with my mouth.

"I should punish you for this," the young CEO whispered, his words harsh but not unkind. And with that, he rammed into me, burying himself deep within my folds. He motioned for Young Sik to join us as I screamed his name . . . their names. When the rapper stuffed himself into my mouth, I felt complete.

Overhead, I heard them kissing again. It drove me wild, and I groped around with one hand, trying to find Jintae and to press his fingers to my clit. He dodged my every attempt. "You don't get to come yet," he admonished. "This is your doing, and you won't come til I say you can."

Then the kissing started again.

Each thrust from Jintae made me swallow Young Sik more. I took more of him into my mouth than I'd ever taken.

Both men's movements became erratic as they came closer to blowing their loads inside me. The flesh between my legs cried out to be touched. Every nerve was alive and begging. If I squeezed my thighs together, I could almost apply enough pressure to feel relief, but not quite.

When Jintae came after one last jam into me, Young Sik soon followed, his cum shooting down my throat. Before I could pull myself away from either man, Jintae disengaged and flung me onto my back. His head dipped between my thighs as he stuck two fingers inside me. I squirmed like a worm on a hook, grabbing his head and mashing it against me as an explosive orgasm jolted through my body. Young Sik smothered my screams with kisses.

And afterward, we collapsed in a heap, fully sated and closer than we'd ever been. If three could become one, we had accomplished that. And we were stronger for it.

Chapter Thirty-One

Wednesday morning, I sat at my desk in my office, my phone sitting beside me. I had no clients today, but I had a lot of photos to edit, like always.

Every little notification chime on my phone sent my heart racing, and I'd pick it up to see if it were an email, for today was the day Kilo would contact the photoshoot winner. This was a big deal to me, because it could steer my career in a whole new direction. Sure, I'd done magazine shoots before, but nothing of this caliber.

I edited another photo and saved it. My phone chimed again. A text alert.

Who was texting me? I gathered up my phone and looked at it.

An unknown number. Was Kilo alerting by text instead? Curious, I opened the message. My eyes darted across the words and I paled. What the hell? What did *he* want?

It's Minhyuk. Meet me at our old café at noon. I have something for you.

When I tried to send a reply to tell him I absolutely would not be meeting him, the message wouldn't send. He'd used a burner phone and had destroyed it already. That worried me. Fuck. I had to go.

I arrived at the café around noon. It was close to our old neighborhood, and we'd gone there almost every Saturday— when he wasn't away on a shoot—until we broke up.

The café owner squealed when she saw me. "Lindsey! What brings you here? I haven't seen you in months!"

I bowed my head to her. "It's nice to see you. I'm actually here to meet someone. I mean, to meet Minhyuk."

"Oh. He rented one of my private rooms, but he hasn't shown up yet. Come on, I'll bring you there."

Even though the café was small, it catered to celebrities since it sat so close to Pyeongchang-dong. Celebrities liked their privacy, so she had three rooms at the back through a doorway that served that purpose. She led me to the one on the far left, Minhyuk's favorite.

"Can I get you something while you wait?" she asked as I removed my shoes and stepped up onto the platform and through the sliding door. A low table sat in the middle of the room, surrounded by cushions.

"No, thank you," I replied. "I don't plan on staying long."

Whatever it was Minhyuk had for me, I was only going to stay long enough to see it, then go.

She nodded and turned to leave, then swiveled back my way. "Lindsey, if you need anything, you know . . . *need*—" she said the word low and drawn out "—just ask me for an iced cappuccino and I'll call the police, okay? You can yell it out. I'll hear it."

I smiled. That made me feel better. "Thank you."

After she left, I settled myself onto one cushion, trying to keep myself calm. This was stupid, I thought. I should have contacted the guys to let them know where I was. But Jintae had two important meetings today, so that only left Young Sik. I pulled my phone out to shoot him a quick text, but the door to the room slid open and Minhyuk stepped inside.

I hadn't seen him in person since the night he threw me out. He was still as handsome as I remembered, but there was a hardness to his stare that sent my heart beating an erratic rhythm in my chest. He looked like he wouldn't hesitate to kill me.

I slipped the phone back in my pocket, no message sent, and stood to give him a respectful bow. I kept the words the café owner has told me on my tongue, ready to shout them if need be. But he merely nodded his head in return and motioned me to sit, taking the cushion opposite me.

"What was it you wanted?" I asked, skipping the pleasantries.

"Can't we order first?" he said and picked up a menu.

"Minhyuk-ssi, I'm a busy woman. I have too much to do to waste my time here with you."

"You will order something and eat with me," he replied, his stare striking fear in my heart. I swallowed. When had he gotten so ruthless?

"Fine," I replied, snatching the menu off of the table and throwing it open. "What are you going to have?"

He dropped his menu, an annoyed look on his face. "What do I always get?"

"I dunno," I said, just to annoy him.

He breathed out sharply through his nose. "It's only been a few months. My tastes haven't changed."

I flicked my eyes his way. "Except, apparently, they have."

His eyes burned over the menu he'd picked back up again. I mirrored his look. He knew what I was talking about, and it pissed him off. Well, I was pissed off as well.

"How is she, by the way?" I asked, forcing pleasantness into my voice . . . or maybe it was sarcasm.

The café owner came in to take our orders. Minhyuk ordered a sandwich and an iced Americano. I ordered a peach-flavored boba tea.

"Aren't you going to order something to eat?" he asked, handing his menu to the owner.

"I told you I'm not here to eat. You called me here because you had something for me. Just show me what it is, so I can go. I have a lot of work to do today and I'm waiting on an important email." I handed the owner my menu, and she left us.

"And I told you, you can take the time to eat with me. Are we just going to bicker in circles now?"

I crossed my arms. "I'll chew on the tapioca balls in my tea while you eat."

We sat in a stony silence until our orders came. Minhyuk took the time to eat half his sandwich while I sipped on my tea, chewing on the tapioca balls as I sucked them up through the straw.

He set his sandwich on the plate and dug out a large envelope from an inside pocket of his jacket. He set it on the table and slid it over to me, keeping his hand on it.

"I was honestly hoping I wouldn't have to do this, but you're acting unreasonable and reminding me why I broke up with you in the first place, so here we are."

A bolt of confusion jolted through me. What was he even talking about? "Minhyuk, I don't understand."

"I want you out of Korea. I can't stand you even being in the same country as me."

"Huh?" The confusion turned to anger. "You have got to be kidding me. I can't move. I have a career. I like it here."

"You being here is ruining my career. You need to go."

"No. Absolutely not." I stood, ignoring the envelope on the table. "I'm leaving." Rage pulsed through me, making my limbs shake.

"Sit. Down." His raised voice startled me, but I wasn't about to spend another moment here. He was crazy if he thought I'd listen to him.

I turned to leave, but he shot to his feet and grabbed my wrist, pulling me toward him. The scent of his cologne assaulted my nose. He pushed me back toward my seat and knocked my feet out from under me, so I crashed back onto the cushion.

"I said, sit down," he repeated. After I reluctantly settled, crossing my arms in defiance once again, he continued. "You will leave Korea. I'll give you a week to get a ticket somewhere else."

"And if I don't?" I jutted my chin out at him.

"Then I'll spread *that*," he pointed to the envelope on the table, "to all the major news outlets."

I frowned at him and picked up the manilla envelope. With my eyes darting from him to the envelope, I opened it and slid out what was inside.

A gasp escaped me.

"How did you—? Where did you get this?" I slid it back. "Minhyuk, where did you get this?!"

He gave me a smug look. "You have a week. You can leave now."

Chapter Thirty-Two

As I headed home, I twisted the envelope in my hands. The taxi seemed to crawl. Frustrated, I pulled out my phone and called Young Sik. I'd already informed Anne I wasn't coming back to the office.

My hands shook as I held the phone up to my ear. Young Sik picked up on the second ring. "*Yeoboseyo?*"

"Young . . ." Suddenly I couldn't speak. Tears threatened. My breath hitched so loudly the taxi driver peeked at me in his mirror.

"Lindsey? What's wrong? Are you okay?" Young Sik asked.

"N-no. I'm not okay. I . . . can you come home? Please?" My voice cracked.

"You're home? I'll be right there."

"Thank you." I hung up.

"Miss, are you okay?" the driver asked, concern worrying his face.

I could only shake my head. "Just take me home." Then I broke down and cried.

I grabbed a beer out of the fridge. I needed something to calm my nerves before Young Sik got here, or else I'd be a blubbering mess.

I was halfway through my second can when the front door slammed open and Young Sik rushed around the corner toward me.

I thought the beer would help me keep my emotions under control, but as soon as I saw him drift around the corner, I lost it and started crying. I threw myself into his arms.

He wrapped himself around me, letting me cry for a few minutes in his cocoon of warmth.

"What happened?" he asked. "Are you hurt?"

I shook my head and sucked in a breath. "No. I'm not hurt. I . . . I got a text from Minhyuk." And I spilled the entire story to him. Afterward, I handed him the envelope.

He slipped the now-crumpled photo out and gasped. "Where did he get this?"

"I don't know."

Young Sik studied it. "At least we're not having sex in this one."

"He has all of them. He told me he'd release them if I didn't buy a . . . ticket . . ." I had to stop. Just the thought of leaving Korea caused tears to threaten again.

"We won't let that happen," Young Sik answered. "And if it does happen, you won't be alone. I'll go with you."

"I don't want to put that burden on you. You have a career here."

194

"As do you. Trust me, Lindsey. I won't let you leave alone. I can write music anywhere.." He looked at the photo once more. "Have you told Jintae?"

"No. With all his meetings today, I knew he'd be busy."

"I'll shoot him a text."

He got a reply a minute later. "He says he'll be able to break away in about an hour."

We retired to the couch. Young Sik turned on the tv, but neither of us watched it. Instead, I wrapped myself in his embrace while he smoothed the hair on my head.

When Jintae came home, I retold the story to him. His eyes were a thin line the whole time. "I'll kill him," he said.

"Why is violence always the answer with you?" Young Sik asked.

"Shall I kill you, too?"

I stepped between them. "Guys, this is not the time for this. We need to come up with something"—I glared at Jintae—"besides killing."

The young CEO pulled his phone from his pocket. "Give me a few minutes. I have an idea." He dialed a number and headed to his room, his voice fast and angry as he walked.

Young Sik and I stared at each other.

Finally I said, "He has one of the best legal teams in the business. If anyone can handle it, Jintae can."

"But doesn't that mean he'll have to reveal our relationship?"

I paled. "Shit."

At that moment, I got an email notification. I'd gotten the Kilo photoshoot.

Chapter Thirty-Three

I felt like this was going to be the final showdown between Minhyuk and me. Jintae had planned everything faster than I imagined. In two days, his team had drafted a cease-and-desist order and had sent out warnings to every influential news outlet in Korea.

Jintae told me when Minhyuk contacted me about sending him proof of me buying a ticket out of Korea, I was to text my ex back to call me. And I was to accept no excuses.

That text from him came Saturday while I was home alone. I immediately replied, *Call me. It's important.*

To be honest, I didn't expect him to do any such thing, so I jumped when the phone rang in my hand.

"*Yeoboseyo?*" I answered, my hands shaking.

"*Ya!* What do you even want, bitch?" The voice on the other end was not Minhyuk but Ji Bong Cha, the woman he'd left me for. I should have known. She was behind all this, was she? Well, I wasn't about to let her intimidate me.

"Put Minhyuk on the phone," I said, using informal speech in return. If she was going to be rude, I could be rude right back.

"He's not here."

"Then pass this on to him, and I'm only going to say it once. Tomorrow night Jintae, Young Sik, and I will come over to discuss this situation with him. He'd better be there or shit will surely hit the fan." I hung up without giving her a chance to retaliate.

Chapter Thirty-Four

Sunday night, we three piled into Jintae's car along with his computer friend, Jinju. Jinju wouldn't be coming inside, but he had an important role this night.

We made the ride to Pyeongchang-dong in silence. Jintae drove, his knuckles white as he gripped the steering wheel. I sat beside him, staring out the window, my heart pounding in my chest. For the hundredth time since leaving, my hand patted my pants pocket where a tiny device lay hidden.

Young Sik and Jinju sat in the back. The car was lit with an eerie glow and tapping sounded as Jinju got his computer ready for his part.

We weren't even sure that Minhyuk would let us in. I had heard nothing from him since I'd talked to that bitch Bong Cha. Not that it mattered. We didn't need to enter Minhyuk's mansion to put our plan into motion. But it would help.

Jintae glanced over at me, his eyes glittering in the subdued light. He reached out and laid his hand on mine as I twisted my fingers in my lap.

"It'll be okay," he said. But he looked just as nervous as I felt.

When we pulled up to the iron gate of Minhyuk's mansion wall, Jintae cut the engine and turned to face us.

"Are we ready?" We each nodded. "Let's do this. Fighting!"

We copied him, shouting, "Fighting!" and pumping our fists down.

I got out of the car first, striding over to the intercom. This was the crucial moment for the plan. Would he let us in or would he play the coward and leave us to Plan B?

I pushed the button and waited. There was no answer, but the gate rumbled open.

Jinju stayed behind us, using us as a cover as we entered the gate. Once we were inside, he separated from us to follow the wall off into the darkness. We continued on our way, keeping our strides confident.

I buzzed the door, and it swung open right away. Bong Cha stood there, her pretty face wrinkled in a scowl. "Do you *really* think this is going to make a difference?" she asked.

I pushed right past her. "We're not here to see you."

Behind me, Jintae snickered.

She huffed. "He's in his office."

"Good," I replied. Exactly where we wanted him.

The guys followed me through the foyer and up the stairs to the second floor. The bedroom wing was on the right. We turned left where a wide, short hall led to a single door. I contemplated just barging in on him, but ultimately knocked.

A muffled voice called out, "Come in!" I twisted the knob and pushed, striding in like I owned the place with Jintae and Young Sik right behind me.

Neither guy could hide his awe at the vastness of the room. Minhyuk's office took up the entire left wing. It was lined ceiling to floor with shelves that held a multitude of books and his prized gem collection. Those were encased in glass.

His desk stood on the far side of the room on a raised dais in front of a wall of glass that had the curtains drawn across.

Minhyuk stood as we entered. He beckoned to us. We stepped up onto the dais and stood in front of the massive desk.

He gave us a curt nod, followed by a smirk. "Ah, is this what is known as a reverse harem? Like those silly novels you like to read?"

On either side of me, the guys shifted and crossed their arms, not taking the bait.

Minhyuk continued. Pointing at Jintae, he said, "You. You, I've seen. But you"—he switched his gaze to Young Sik—"I don't believe we've met."

"Choi Young Sik," the rapper said. He hid his normal genial appearance behind a facade of stoicism. He could look fierce when he wanted to, and Minhyuk withered under his glare.

"Let's get to the point," I said. I pulled out a small jump drive that doubled as a secret microphone so Jinju could listen in. It recorded everything onto his laptop. "Just transfer the photos on here for me and we'll leave." I slammed the drive on the desk, knowing full well he wouldn't comply.

Minhyuk cocked his head. "Did you buy the ticket?"

"I'm not leaving."

He shook his head. "Then you're not getting the photos. Oh, watching you three fall will bring so much joy to me." A grin split his face.

Jintae pulled an envelope from his jacket and placed it on the desk.

"What's this?" my ex asked.

"The reason we're here. It's a cease-and-desist order."

Minhyuk laughed. "Do you think that will stop me? Go ahead. Sue me all you want. When everyone sees the photos, you'll go down in flames so fast you won't get the chance to sue me."

"You think we're only sending this to you?" Jintae asked. "My legal team has already sent letters to all the major networks and celebrity sites warning them of the consequences if they publish anything you send them. And they are to report any photos to the police as stolen property."

The grin slid off Minhyuk's face. He turned his attention back to me. "Are you really taking part in this? It's disgusting, you know."

"What I do behind closed doors is my own business. I will neither acknowledge nor deny my actions. And I'm not leaving Korea."

In my earpiece, I heard Jinju's voice. "Got it."

"Come on, guys," I said. "Let's go."

Minhyuk got a panicked look on his face. "Wait!"

I stopped and turned his way.

"Can I speak to you . . . in private?" he asked, eyeing the guys.

I sighed. To them I said, "I'll meet you outside." They raised their eyebrows but did not question me.

Once we were alone, I asked, "So what's this all about, really? You know I'm not hurting you. It's been months. Why now?"

He sighed, like he had an intense weight on him he needed to discard. "Bong Cha feels threatened. She doesn't want you here anymore."

"Bong Cha? Why? What did I ever do to her?"

"Before she was an actress, she was a photographer."

"Okay. So?"

"She lost out to you on that drama I filmed in America."

"So, what . . . is this some pitiful act of revenge on me? Is that why she's with you?"

"I found out about it afterward. After she and I got together. By then I was in too deep to refuse her."

"Bullshit!" My anger flared. "You could have stopped it at any time. You could have asked me for help. All you had to do was say something. Instead, you destroyed my property and tried to ruin me!"

He hung his head. The bravado from earlier drained from him. I realized his previous nastiness had been an act . . . orchestrated by her.

"Just give me the photos, Minhyuk. Let's end this now."

"Are you really with both guys?" he asked.

I didn't answer him. Instead, I stormed out. I was done.

As we left the mansion, Jinju caught up with us. We didn't say a word until we got into the car and pulled away.

"So, it's done?" Young Sik asked the computer hacker.

"Oh yeah. When he opens the files, they'll all be the same. Just the one you told me to use." The photo in question was the very same one Minhyuk had shown to blackmail me. Me sitting in between the guys, all of us scantily clad. If it ever got out, we could easily dismiss it as a photoshoot for the Kilo promotion.

"Were there anymore copies?" I asked.

"Not that I could see unless he had them stored on a jump drive or has hard copies of them. I checked his computers and his phone and changed all I saw." He held up a finger, listening. He still had in an earpiece connected to the jump drive/listening device I'd left on Minhyuk's desk.

"Oh shit. That girl's yelling at him. Hang on." He flipped his laptop open, and it flashed to life. "Let me replay this bit for you."

As we drove home, we listened to Bong Cha chew Minhyuk out about not keeping any extra copies of the photos after they realized what Jinju had done to the files.

Our plan had worked better than expected.

Epilogue

Six Months Later

Young Sik was balls-deep inside me when the bedroom door burst open. We both swung our heads that way as Jintae strode into the room. He stopped, staring at us for a moment before exclaiming, "Starting without me? I still need to take a shower."

Young Sik raised up on his arms. "Sorry, man. We weren't expecting you back yet."

Jintae's forehead furrowed for a moment, his face darkening, before he laughed and rubbed the back of his head. "I'll just shower then."

The guys didn't always get along. Even six months after we'd thwarted Minhyuk's plan to ruin us, they still had their moments of jealousy, hissing at each other like angry cats. But, mostly, they were closer than brothers.

The next few weeks were going to be busy for us. Jintae and Young Sik were working on their first collaboration album. The single they'd produced earlier had been a hit, leaving the fans wanting more. They were happy to oblige. Both were excited to start recording, and the little snippets they'd let me hear sounded amazing.

I had won the opportunity to shoot for Kilo and that was happening soon, too, after a few months of delays due to their star model getting in an accident.

When Jintae emerged from the shower, Young Sik was sitting on the edge of the bed, his head thrown back and groaning as I sucked him off.

Jintae came up behind me as I sat on the floor and pulled my hips toward him. He slipped inside me without a word. I felt his hands on my shoulders as he leaned over my back. Young Sik shifted forward, and I glanced up in time to see their lips connect, Jintae's hand wrapped around the back of Young Sik's head. Their kiss was so passionate I clenched Jintae's dick with my walls, making him moan into Young Sik's mouth.

I tore my eyes away to concentrate on Young Sik's dick. With Jintae kissing him, it didn't take long for him to come, coating the back of my throat. He pulled out and flopped backward on the bed, his chest rising and falling with his heavy breathing. "Goddamn," he whispered, grinning from ear to ear with his eyes closed.

Jintae pulled out and flipped me to face him. "Sit up on the bed between Young Sik's legs," he told me. Then to the rapper, "Hold her, man."

The way he said it made me gush.

Young Sik sat back up, and I settled between his naked thighs, my ass balanced on the edge of the bed. Jintae stood and positioned himself in front of me, his bed the perfect height so he could enter me. He put his hands on my hips to steady me. I raised my legs and wrapped them around his waist as he thrust inside me.

Young Sik ran his tongue around my earlobe. I groaned until Jintae silenced me with his lips. Young Sik nibbled on my ear. In response, I tangled my fingers in Jintae's hair and deepened the kiss.

One of Young Sik's arms wrapped around my chest to keep me in place. The other slid downward until his fingers found my clit. With a sharp intake of air, I thrust my hips forward, causing Jintae to sink deeper into me with each thrust. It didn't take long for the tension to build, and his lips could silence me no more. I cried out as an orgasm rocked my body. My muscles clenched Jintae so tightly he grunted and thrust faster until he shot his seed deep inside my womb.

Afterward we lay in a heap on the bed, me still in Young Sik's arms with Jintae's wrapped around both of us. Jintae alternated kisses between me and Young Sik until we dozed off, content in our embraces.

I don't know how long this will last between us. It may last forever, or there may come a day when one of us doesn't want to do it anymore. Nothing is for certain, anyway. Even monogamous relationships can end after decades of togetherness. Ours might not be any different. But right now, I don't care. We are happy and we are together, and, dammit, I'm going to enjoy every minute while it lasts.

END